ZALA

O.L OBONNA

Pageleaf Publishing

www.pageleafpublishing.com

First Pageleaf Publishing Electronic Edition: March 2025 ISBN (Paperback): 978-1-7392841-0-7

First Pageleaf Publishing Print Edition: March 2025 Cover design by Sutabal Mondal

Printed in the United Kingdom

© 2025 O.L. Obonna

Books By O.L Obonna

Forever And a Day

When Love Lasts

Yahimba

Coming Soon

Obehi

A Season to Begin again

Wedding Wahala

Bound by His Legacy

The List

Buried Secrets, Broken Scars

Entangled Hearts

For Dorothy Obonna

The Lagos Elite Club

Meet Eyimofe, Tseye and Naade

They met and bonded at university, and a brotherhood was formed. In the years since they graduated, they have made their mark in their respective careers and earned reputations as hardworking and wealthy playboys, wreaking havoc on the female population in Lagos, Nigeria.

Their Motto: "Work hard and play hard."

They have it all: wealth, looks and ladies; life is good, or is it? Yet nothing is as straightforward as it looks. Everything goes according to plan until these resolute bachelors finally meet the women who turn their whole worlds upside down.

Meet Yahimba, Zala and Obehi

The women who have these most sought-after bachelors desperate to say, "I DO."

They are beautiful, independent, strong-willed, and determined not to be taken for a ride.

1

PROLOGUE

Bole, Addis Ababa

A week ago, my ex-husband signed the divorce papers. After three years of torture, I am finally free!

Free from a prison of a marriage, free from him! Oh God, I am finally free!

I can't believe I gave up the love of my life to marry for power, to please my family. I married that monster because everybody said it was the right thing to do. They said, who marries for love when you are from a family of diplomats?

My scars will always remind me of how foolish I was to think that marrying Negasi Abeba was the best thing to do and to think I gave up Tseye for it. I will always regret my actions, but I can do nothing about the past.

My father has just been posted back to Nigeria as the

Ethiopian Deputy Head of Mission to Nigeria. I have decided to accompany my parents to start a new life.

I hurt, I hurt a lot, especially when I see the scar above my eye, but I wear it with pride as it proves that I am a survivor.

I have been scarred by love, but I survived.

It is time for me to take a step forward and leave it all behind. I must let go and believe I can start afresh. I have to believe Negasi Abeba didn't ruin me but gave me the will and strength to survive.

I have to do it for Zuri and myself. I can do it, and I will do it.

I am Zala Kebede.

Chapter One

Zala reached up and scratched the top of her right eyelid. Her scars were itching again, which caused her major concern. Reaching for her handbag, she searched for the ointment the family doctor had recommended. The bandages had come off a couple of weeks ago, and she was glad for that.

Walking around Addis Ababa with a patch over one eye had been embarrassing, to say the least; thank goodness the plasters had come off.

Her best friend Lola had been livid when the doctor had told her the scar would not fade. But Zala had been happy to have the scar as a reminder of her stupidity. Sighing, she reached for the bottle of water in her weekend bag.

She took a mouthful of cold water from it as the car carrying her raced towards Ikoyi, heading away from the hustle and bustle of Muritala Mohammed International Airport.

Lagos.

She had not been back in four years. The city unfurled around her, a chaotic mosaic of sound and color. Hawkers weaved through the sluggish traffic, their voices rising above the honking horns and the low rumble of engines.

Lagos.

The last time she was here, she had left her heart behind. She remembered standing at Murtala Muhammed International Airport, eyes dry and swollen from crying, lips pressed into a thin line, as she prepared to return home to Addis Ababa,

Tseye Harriman.

His name slipped through her mind, soft and sharp, like the edge of a well-worn blade. She let herself drift back to the years when his name had meant home. When just the brush of his fingers against hers could light up her entire world.

She wondered what he was doing now.

He was probably married with kids now; Tseye was too hot a catch to remain single for a long time: he and his friends, Eyimofe and Naade.

She smiled as she thought of her time with them in London and Lagos, the happiest she had ever been. She had thought those friendships would last a long time.

Friendships that she had destroyed.

* * *

"We are here, Zala," her mother's soft voice woke her. "Oh," she said as she sat up straight, surprised at how quick the trip from the airport had been. "That was quick," she added, stretching and stifling a yawn. The ache of the long flight still clung to her, a dull heaviness in her bones. "Zuri?" she asked her mum, looking around for her daughter, who had chosen to go with her mother in a different vehicle.

"She's already rushed into the house to pick a room." Mariam Kebede, Zala's mum, chuckled as they exited the vehicle and walked towards the imposing white house that would be her home for the foreseeable future.

Zala smiled as she thought of Zuri.

Zuri was the sole reason she had remained sane, and the only reason she had decided enough was enough.

"Smart girl." She smiled as they walked into the foyer, where they were greeted by a group of people she assumed were the house management staff.

Looking around, she tried to ignore her bitterness toward her parents but couldn't, which was unfair because, deep down, she knew they were not the reason she was a shadow of her former self.

She had decided to leave Tseye.

Four years ago, she had not been brave enough to fight for him and refuse Negasi's proposal. Her parents wanted her to marry Negasi, but deep down, Zala knew that if she had refused, her parents would have supported her.

But she didn't refuse Negasi's proposal because she didn't want to hinder her father's career. Her father had always wanted to become Deputy Head of Mission, so she married Negasi. Theirs was a political marriage that paved the way for her father's career.

Well, he had gotten his wish.

Her father finally became a Deputy Head of Mission to a West African country. The only reason she had chosen to accompany her parents to Nigeria was because they had come through for her when they found out what she'd been going through. Her father had almost killed Negasi; he had practically held him down and forced him to sign the divorce papers and waive all rights to their daughter, Zuri.

Negasi had refused, and the case was still in the family court in Addis Ababa.

He had agreed to the divorce but was contesting custody of their daughter.

She shook her head as she remembered how adamant he had been when she told him she was travelling and Zuri would go with her, pending the family court's decision.

She had threatened him before he allowed her to travel with Zuri.

The divorce was only possible because her father had intervened, and if it were the last thing she did, she would ensure he had no access to Zuri.

Her parents not only ensured the divorce happened but also brought her to accompany them here because they were worried about her.

Her father also contacted fellow diplomats and got her a job in Lagos; she was grateful for that.

She was starting a new life here.

A new life with her daughter Zuri, away from the horror of her marriage. She was worried about running into Tseye because she wasn't sure how to face him after what she had done to him.

Who was she kidding?

She didn't want to run into him with a wife and kids in tow, it would hurt her to see that.

But she knew she needed to see Tseye.

* * *

Tseye Harriman sat parked outside his half-sister's house,

his mind preoccupied as he waited to take her to his friend's birthday bash at Eko Hotel. The evening was already unfolding, but Yahimba had yet to appear.

Despite the repeated invitations, she hadn't returned to his parents' house for a second dinner. It weighed on him, but he refused to push her on the matter. He knew better than to force it, especially with everything that had transpired recently. Yahimba would come when she was ready; he had to trust that. He'd give her the space she needed, even if it meant waiting a little longer. They had only met a couple of weeks ago when his father informed him and his mother of her existence. His mother had been hurt; he, on the other hand, had been excited to find out that he had a sister and was determined to get to know her.

This was their second outing together; he had taken her to íte the first time, and now he was here to pick her up to attend Naade's party held at Eko Hotel.

He smiled and waved her over as she exited her building.

"Hey, you." He grinned as Yahimba got into his car.

She flashed him a smile, her brown eyes twinkling with mischief.

"Can you stop by the mall so I can get a gift for Naade?" she asked.

"What for? I didn't buy him a gift; why should you?" Tseye grinned as she threw him a surprised look, muttering

9

something about stingy people under her breath.

Tseye smiled as they chatted while they drove to the Eko Hotel.

He was already running late and knew Naade would be frustrated when he eventually showed up. A small sigh escaped his lips as he thought of his best friends, Eyimofe Alele - Williams and Naade Adekoya - Phillips.

For over ten years, they'd been through thick and thin together, their bond forged through shared experiences, laughter, and countless late nights. What had started as a simple friendship evolved into something more profound when they co-founded their first company. They worked tirelessly and played even harder; through every high and low, they remained unshakably close.

Their relationship thrived because of the respect they had for each other.

Naade and the others were already gathered at the pool-side bar when Tseye and Yahimba arrived. The air was alive with the soft hum of conversation, punctuated by the clinking of glasses and the occasional burst of laughter. Overhead, the faint sound of water splashing mingled with the distant music playing from the speakers.

"We are over by the bar," Tseye said, his voice clear and confident as he cut through the buzz of the crowd.

He gestured toward the group, nudging Yahimba gently

as he led her through the crowd.

Tseye's eyes immediately found Naade and Eyimofe. They were standing together, caught up in a conversation that was clearly filled with shared history. Their laughter rose above the general chatter, a sound so familiar and warm that it seemed to draw in everyone around them.

Naade saw them approaching and broke into a broad smile, his expression warm and welcoming.

"You made it, and you brought Yahimba," Naade said, walking towards them.

Tseye nodded, turning to face Eyimofe, who stood with an outstretched hand.

With a firm handshake, Tseye greeted his longtime friend, the two of them exchanging a quick, knowing smile as they locked eyes. Behind him, Naade and Yahimba were already deep in conversation.

A burst of laughter broke out as Naade, with his usual playful insistence, urged Yahimba to call him by his first name. "Come on, Yahimba," he teased, "You're family now. No more of this formal stuff."

Tseye chuckled at the scene, watching as Yahimba gave Naade an exasperated but amused look. "Fine, Naade," she said with a dramatic sigh.

"What are you drinking?" Tseye asked. "I'm heading to the bar."

"Any juice would be fine," his sister replied as he turned and walked towards the bar to order their drinks, leaving the others chatting.

Glancing back at her, Tseye felt a quiet sense of relief, that she had agreed to come out with him tonight, but there was still more work to be done to get her to accept his parents, especially his father.

Baby steps, he reminded himself; Yahimba would come around, eventually, she had too.

As he turned back toward the bar to collect the drinks he had ordered, his mind briefly wandered to the task ahead.

But the moment he reached for the glasses, something or rather, someone caught his eye and he stiffened, looking up.

It was her.

He would know her anywhere. His heart skipped a beat, the rush of emotions hitting him like a tidal wave. She stood on the far side of the pool, just a few paces away from Eyimofe and Zala. Her presence somehow drew his attention with an intensity that was hard to shake.

The lights from the pool shimmered across the water, casting a soft glow on her figure, and for a moment, the buzz of the crowd faded into a distant hum.

Tseye's gaze locked on her, and his breath quickened as shock rolled through him. It felt like time had stopped, almost slowed. For a heartbeat, the noise of the party seemed to fade into the back- ground.

It was her, Zala Kebede, his cheating, selfish ex. Zala Kebede, the one woman who had broken him down completely.

Zala Kebede, the only woman he had ever loved.

She was hard to miss.

She looked amazing, her presence commanding attention. Her dress hugged her figure in all the right places, and her beauty stood out like a beacon, drawing his eyes to her no matter how hard he tried to look away.

Tseye felt it.

He felt a pull in his chest, a familiar ache he thought he had buried. It had been years but seeing her again... God.

She still looked the same. Zala Kebede, what the hell was she doing here, in Lagos? And was she here with her husband? To remind him of what he had lost when she walked out on him.

Fate couldn't be so cruel, could it?

After four years together, she had walked away only to marry someone else just weeks later. Tseye could never understand why she had done it. It was as if everything they had shared meant nothing, and that had broken him.

Had it not been for Eyimofe, Naade and Misan, he would

never have gotten over her.

Seeing her standing there, his mind couldn't help but race. What was she doing here? His gaze locked onto her across the pool as if some invisible force had tethered him to her.

The world around him seemed to blur, the party chatter fading into the background as his focus homed in on Zala. Their eyes met, and for a split second, everything stopped.

Her eyes widened, a flash of alarm crossing her face, and in that instant, the flood of anger and hurt he'd buried for years came rushing back.

His pulse quickened, his chest tightening.

Zala.

Damn her.

Tseye couldn't let her see the effect she still had on him, couldn't give her the satisfaction of knowing how deeply she had hurt him, when she walked away. He grabbed the drinks he'd ordered, his fingers tightening around the cool glasses as if it were the only thing keeping him grounded. His jaw clenched, a subtle ripple of muscle beneath his skin, and without another glance, he turned on his heel, each step measured and brisk as he made his way back to Yahimba.

"Tseye," Yahimba began, but he handed her the drinks, squeezing her arms.

"Give me a moment Yahimba. I need to get some air," he whispered into her ear. "Please?"

Yahimba nodded, and without a word, he turned and strode away, his head pounding.

What the hell was she doing here?

The question exploded in his mind, his jaw tightening as he took in the sight of her.

This was a public place, but if she had any ounce of decency left, she would've kept her distance, ignored him, and ignored his friends.

But there she was, standing a few paces from them.

Her presence was like a sharp reminder of everything he had lost.

His mind spiraled.

Who could ever understand women's reasoning?

One moment, they are walking away, leaving you in pieces, and the next, they are right back in your space, acting like nothing ever happened.

The nerve.

Chapter Two

Zala felt as though she'd been stabbed, the sharp sting of his disregard cutting through her as Tseye turned away without so much as a glance.

Well, what had she expected? That he would smile and hug her like they were friends? Forcing a smile, she turned to face Eyimofe, and the young lady Tseye had just spoken to, who was probably the woman in his life.

She was beautiful.

Zala felt a sharp pang of envy as the young lady turned to watch Eyimofe walk away, a worried look on her face.

"Eyimofe," Zala greeted, her voice a touch uncertain but soft, the years between them evident in the way she said his name.

"Zala, it's been a while." Eyimofe replied, his tone flat, not quite warm, but not cold either.

As she stood there, trying to collect herself, her eyes caught

Naade standing a few paces away. Naade wasn't even looking in her direction, acknowledging her. Zala felt a sharp pang of hurt, a reminder of how her actions had pushed her out of their circle. Her lips tightened, the muscles in her jaw clenched with a mixture of frustration and sorrow.

Her fingers dug into her palms, the pressure grounding her, as if trying to keep herself from saying or doing something she might regret. Eyimofe's distant tone and Naade's obvious coldness stung more than she wanted to admit. She had never been good at hiding her emotions, but today, standing among them, she fought to keep her composure. The old familiarity between them felt like a distant echo, like it belonged to another lifetime.

There's no point standing here, she thought bitterly. No point in making small talk with Tseye's friends when they won't even acknowledge me.

"It was nice to see you, Eyimofe," she said.

"You too," Eyimofe replied, his tone guarded, eyes careful.

"You don't mean that, Eyimofe." Her face was tinged with sadness as she looked past Eyimofe to Naade, who had turned to look in the direction, Tseye had disappeared to. "You don't mean that; say hi to Naade." She repeated. "And Tseye, too." With a nod at Yahimba, she turned and walked away, her heart heavy as she moved towards her parents, who were sitting and chatting with old friends.

She had been so excited and eager to return to Nigeria, to leave her home country and move away from all that had made her life miserable.

Now, she wondered if returning to Nigeria was a wise decision.

Especially after seeing Tseye and his friends.

"Are you okay?" her mother asked as she sat beside her.

Reaching under the table to squeeze her mother's hand, she nodded.

"Yes, I am."

"Zala?"

"Mum, I'm fine." She squeezed her mother's hand to reassure her even as her heart shattered into a million pieces.

* * *

He didn't want to remember the past but seeing her had brought too many painful memories back.

"Hey Tseye, are you okay?"

Tseye turned to find Naade standing behind him.

"I'm fine. Seeing Zala again had caught me off guard. I was shocked, and walking away was the best thing to do.

"I understand. Are you good, though?" Naade insisted.

"You want the truth? I don't know, and I can't tell you if

I'm okay. Zala is the last person I expected to see in Lagos. She is supposed to be in Addis Ababa, happily married," Tseye replied bitterly.

"Don't do that to yourself, Tseye. It's not worth it, and again, she has always loved Lagos, so of course, she would come back and visit at some point."

"She hasn't visited in four years, Naade."

"And you know that how?" asked Naade.

"We have mutual friends. We would have heard if she'd come back. Besides, you know I was the reason she came to Nigeria in the first place."

Naade shook his head slowly. "Tseye?"

Tseye smiled, but it didn't reach his eyes. "I'm fine, Naade. Really. I was just caught off guard. Don't worry about it."

He waved off his friend's concern, though the tightness in his chest told a different story. "You go ahead. I need a couple of minutes to myself."

Naade hesitated, eyes searching his friend's face for something, but after a beat, he nodded and turned back towards the pool, blending in with their friends.

Tseye stayed rooted to the spot, his thoughts lingering on Zala for a moment before he exhaled slowly, trying to shake off the emotions swirling inside him.

Hands in his pants pockets, Tseye allowed his thoughts to shift to the last time he had seen Zala, to the day she had told him that it was over. He closed his eyes as regret washed over him. He had been going to propose to her that day, but she hadn't even given him the chance.

When he had asked her why she was so cold towards him, she had said; "I want out, Tseye. This relationship, it's choking me."

He could still remember the shock he had felt.

"I don't love you anymore.", Zala had told him.

Tseye had never forgotten her words.

The next couple of months had been hell; he had replayed her words over and over again as he drank himself into a stupor while she had moved on quickly, getting married within a couple of weeks.

Thankfully, Naade, Eyimofe and Misan had been there for him.

Especially Misan.

Misan had shown up to his apartment, weeks after Zala had broken up with him and, despite the protest of his friends, had emptied a bucket of cold water over him as he lay in bed, drunk and out of it.

Then, to the shock of Eyimofe and Naade, she had dragged him out of bed by his feet and practically kicked him into the bathroom to clean up.

"You stink," Misan said, slamming the door on him.

Thinking of how it had looked to his friends as tiny Misan had shoved and prodded him till he had come to his senses, he smiled.

Thank God for her.

And now, the woman who had driven him to the brink was back in Lagos. What the hell was she doing here? He couldn't wrap his head around it. She was gone by the time he rejoined his friends by the pool, leaving nothing but a lingering, uncomfortable silence in her wake.

Yahimba stood beside Eyimofe, her posture tense, her eyes scanning the crowd.

Eyimofe, however, looked downright irritated, his brow furrowed as if he was just as unsettled by the situation as Tseye.

"You good?" Eyimofe asked quietly.

"Yeah, I am. She took me by surprise, that's all." Eyimofe nodded towards the other side of the bar.

"Heads up, I think she's sitting over there, having dinner with some friends."

Tseye didn't respond right away. He simply turned on his heel and walked towards Naade, ignoring the slight tightening in his chest. The urge to walk up to her, to

21

demand an explanation, was almost overpowering.

But he ignored it, he wasn't going to give her the chance to see how seeing her had rattled him.

Not when she had walked out on him without looking back.

"What's the deal with your sister and Eyimofe?" Naade asked his tone light but his eyes curious. "If looks could kill, Eyimofe would be dead by now."

Tseye's jaw tightened, the question momentarily pulling him from his swirling thoughts. "I have no idea," he replied, sighing heavily.

He glanced back over his shoulder, towards where Zala was sitting with people, his eyes lingering on her. Jeez! Just thinking of her, left him struggling to breathe.

What was she doing here? After all this time...

He swallowed hard, pushing away the onslaught of questions and turned to Naade, forcing a light-hearted tone. "Hey, it's your birthday, alright? Let's not let anything ruin the vibe."

"Sure, man," Naade said, raising an eyebrow, clearly sensing the shift in his friend's mood.

Tseye nodded, offering Naade a brief, strained smile, the kind that barely reached his eyes. He didn't have the energy for more. With a quick nod at Yahimba, he turned and walked away from the poolside, heading toward the restaurant where their friends were already digging into the buffet.

Yahimba followed quietly, her steps measured beside his. They joined the others, but for Tseye, the weight of the moment didn't lift. It hung in the air like a dark cloud, unspoken, heavy and pressing down on him with each step he took. His mind churned with confusion, anger, and a sense of betrayal that refused to fade.

Seeing Zala again, after all this time, stirred something in him, something raw and unfinished.

He could barely focus on his friends as they joked and laughed around the buffet, his thoughts too consumed by the sudden, unexpected return of someone who had shattered his heart when she walked away.

And now she was back.

The thought of it alone was enough to send Tseye's mind into overdrive. His heart raced as he tried to focus, tried to push the images of her from his thoughts. It's Naade's birthday, he reminded himself. It's not about her. But no matter how hard he tried, Zala's face kept creeping into his mind, how could he not think about her?

Zala Kebede had once been his life, the bane of his existence. She had been the woman he imagined his future with, the one he saw himself growing old with.

But all of that had shattered four years ago when she had ended their relationship without so much as an explanation. She had walked into his apartment, calm and businesslike, and casually dropped the bombshell that what they had was nothing more than a "fling."

Fury erupted inside him at the mere thought of it.

He remembered that day so clearly, the shock that had paralyzed him, the pain that had settled deep in his chest, he would never forget.

She had made him feel like a fool.

The woman he had trusted with his heart had torn it to pieces and walked away without a second glance. And now, here she was again, in the same city, after all this time.

Zala Kebede.

The woman he had loved and lost.

The woman who had broken him.

* * *

Four Years Ago

"Hey," Tseye said softly, opening his apartment door to let Zala in.

The moment she stepped inside, he closed the door behind

her and, without thinking, pulled her into his arms.

"I've been waiting for you all day," he murmured softly. "Eyimofe and Naade will be here in a minute." He pulled back slightly to look at her, his brow furrowing. "What's up? You look... worried."

Zala didn't immediately answer.

She stepped out of his embrace; her body language closed off as she folded her arms across her chest.

"I have to return home to Addis Ababa," she said, her voice quiet, almost too calm.

Tseye's heart skipped a beat.

The words hit him harder than he expected. He swallowed. "Yes, we spoke about that weeks ago," he replied, stepping closer to her. "Your father's fiftieth is coming up, but you did say you would return almost immediately after, so what's going on? Why the sudden change in tone?"

Zala's gaze shifted, not meeting his. For a moment, she seemed lost in thought, and Tseye's pulse quickened. Something was off. He could feel it in the air between them, the tension that had settled in as if the space itself were holding its breath. "Is something wrong?" he pressed on softly. "Zala, you're scaring me."

Zara hesitated as though weighing the decision to tell him whatever had been weighing on her heart. Finally, she sighed, her shoulders slumping under whatever weight she was carrying.

"It's not that simple, Tseye," she said quietly. "I've been thinking about everything, about us."

His chest tightened again. "What about us?"

His mind raced. "Are you breaking up with me?"

"No," Zala spoke. "It's not that. But…" She trailed off, unable to finish the sentence.

Tseye reached out, gently cupping her face with one hand, forcing her to meet his gaze. "But what?" he asked, his voice barely above a whisper. He needed to understand.

He needed to know where this was going before his mind spiraled further.

"I've just been feeling… overwhelmed," she said. "The distance, the expectations, my family… all of it. Tseye, I don't know how to balance everything. I'm not sure I can anymore."

A knot twisted in his stomach at her words, but he refused to let his panic rise. "Zala, we've made it work so far. We can make it work." He reached for her hands, holding them tightly. "I'm not asking you to choose between me and your family, but don't shut me out. We can face this together. Whatever it is, we will figure it out."

Zala's eyes searched his for a long moment, and he saw the

conflict within her.

She opened her mouth to speak, but no words came out. Instead, she pulled away slightly, turning her gaze to the floor. "I don't know, Tseye," she whispered. I don't know how to say this to you, and I'm worried about how you will react."

She looked up as the silence stretched between them.

When she said nothing, he stepped towards her. "Zala, what's wrong?"

"When I leave, I'm not coming back to Nigeria."

Her reply wasn't what he wanted to hear, but he forced himself to remain calm as she turned and walked further into his apartment. He followed her quietly, watching as she walked around his living room, looking at pictures of them.

"Zala?"

She turned to face him.

"Please, don't make this hard for me, Tseye." She pleaded her voice breaking.

"What are you talking about, Zala? And how am I making things difficult for you?"

"Tseye, I am getting married." Tseye staggered back.

"Getting married? What are you talking about?"

"Oh God, Tseye!" Zala suddenly snapped, her voice breaking with frustration and pain. "I just told you I'm returning home and getting married. Connect the dots, will you?"

Her words hit him like a slap, and Tseye froze, the blood draining from his face. He stared at her, disbelief and confusion mixing in his chest, knotting his stomach.

He could barely breathe.

"Married?" The word escaped him in a barely audible whisper, like a question he wasn't even sure he wanted the answer to.

Zala's shoulders slumped, her chest rising and falling rapidly with each heavy breath.

"I don't understand," Tseye murmured, his voice so quiet it almost cracked.

He took a step forward, then another, stopping just a few feet away from her. The space between them felt as vast as an ocean, although they stood so close.

"What are you saying, Zala?" he asked softly, his voice thick with emotion.

His mind raced, trying to piece together what she had just thrown at him. "I... don't understand Zala."

Her lips trembled as she looked away, unable to meet his gaze for a moment.

When she finally did, there was no avoiding the sorrow in her eyes, the kind of sorrow he had feared but never expected to see from her.

"I'm sorry, Tseye," she whispered, her voice raw with emotion. "I never wanted to hurt you, but I can't do this anymore. I can't keep living like this; this thing between us has to end. I have to go home. I must be with my family to do what is expected of me."

Her words sliced through him like a blade; he felt like she was twisting a knife in his heart, and he couldn't speak for a moment, he shook his head slowly, watching her in shock, then he cleared his throat.

"Married?" he repeated, the word tasting bitter on his tongue. "You're getting married... to someone else?"

Zala nodded, her eyes never leaving his.

"I have no choice, Tseye," she said softly. "My family and my future are all tied up in this. I thought I could have both, but I can't. Not anymore."

Tseye felt as though the ground beneath him had been pulled away. Everything that had made sense, everything that had felt so solid, was now crumbling into dust.

"No... you can't be serious," he said, his voice growing more desperate, the tremor in his hands betraying the calm he was trying to hold onto. "Zala, this isn't you. You're not the woman who would walk away from what we have."

"I'm not walking away from us," she whispered. "But I am walking towards something else. Something I need to do for myself. For my family. I hope you can understand that."

Tseye took a deep breath, his chest tightening. He felt like his head was about to explode. She couldn't be serious. He had always believed that love could conquer everything.

But now, he wasn't so sure.

"Then why did you come back here?" he demanded. "Why come back to me if you knew you would just leave me? Why move back to Nigeria if you knew there was no hope for us? Four years together, Zala, and you think it's fair to just walk away?"

Zala closed her eyes briefly, a tear slipping down her cheek. "I never meant for this to happen, Tseye.".

Tseye stared at her for a long moment, his heart aching in ways he hadn't known were possible.

"I'm sorry, Tseye," Zala whispered again as she reached for his hand, but he pulled away.

He watched her as she closed her eyes; when she opened them, her eyes were bright with unshed tears.

"It's over, Tseye, and it was fun while it lasted; I am getting married."

"You call four years of us being together fun while it

lasted? Are you being serious?"

"Tseye, please don't make this harder than it is."

"Zala, the last time you were here, in my bed, we were making plans to spend the rest of our lives together!"

She had the grace to look shamefaced as she looked away from him, her eyes shining bright. "Plans change, Tseye. I'm getting married; I just came to tell you I will leave Nigeria this weekend. Please, Tseye, this is already hard for me; don't make it worse," she said as her voice broke.

Tseye reached for her, but she moved out of his reach and crossed the living room.

"Why are you doing this, Zala?" he asked when she turned away.

Tseye felt his world crumble around him as he reached for the small black box in his pocket, his fingers trembling slightly around the ring he had intended to propose with. The weight of the moment crushed him, this was a joke, she had to be joking.

"Zala," he began, but shook her head, not looking at him.

Her next words broke his heart to pieces.

"I'm sorry, Tseye, but what we have was never meant to last. We have different dreams and aspirations, and it's time we end this thing between us."

"You don't mean that, Zala," Tseye forced himself to speak

when he only wanted to shake her and ask her what was wrong with her.

"I just came to tell you that I was leaving. I owe you that."

"Wait," he said when she would have walked out of his apartment. Taking a deep breath, he said quietly, "I love you, Zala, and I won't accept that all this was just a game to you." He watched slowly as she turned to face him and said quietly.

"Love is not always enough, Tseye," she whispered, her voice barely audible, like a plea that fell on deaf ears.

Tseye wanted to weep. She wasn't just leaving him; she was leaving the very foundation of what they had built. He stood frozen, staring at her, his heart shattering with each passing second and word she uttered.

"Take care, Tseye," she added, her gaze drifting to the floor as if she couldn't bear to meet his eyes anymore. She sounded so composed and calm, but he could hear the tremor in her voice and the unspoken hurt beneath her words. "And give my regards to Naade and Eyimofe."

Her words hung in the air like a fragile thread, shredding his last hope.

This was it.

Zala really was leaving.

Without waiting for a response, Zala turned away.

Her steps were measured and deliberate, yet they echoed in slow motion, as though the world around him had paused for one final moment.

Tseye's chest tightened, his hands clenched into fists, but his body refused to move.

He wanted to call her back.

He wanted to shout, to beg, to demand she stay. He wanted to beg her to stay and continue loving him.

But he didn't.

The words wouldn't come. What was left to say?

Thinking back, Tseye wondered why seeing her had unsettled him so much.

Why did he still feel angry and hurt on seeing her?

Zala Kebede was a selfish human being who was not worth thinking about.

Chapter Three

Zala waited for the car to roll to a stop in the parking lot before she exited it, pulling Zuri behind her.

"Where are we, Mum?" an excited Zuri asked as she skipped alongside her mother.

"You wanted to eat waffles, didn't you?" her mum chuckled.

"Yes, but this doesn't look like a cafe," Zuri pointed out.

"Yeah? What does a café look like?"

"Lots of chairs and tables, with plenty of ice cream images on the wall."

"It may have that, we won't know until we get in" her mother replied, shaking her head with a laugh.

"It does? What's it called?" Zuri squealed, her voice filled with excitement as she and her mother walked towards the building, her eyes wide with curiosity.

"The Flowershop Cafe" Zala replied.

"Oh, I like the name, Mummy," Zuri said, her face lighting up as she spoke, her big brown eyes sparkling with curiosity. She tilted her head thoughtfully. "Do they have nice waffles like the ones we eat in **Wafels & Dinges**?" she asked, referring to her favorite Waffle Café back in New York. "You always take me there when we go on holiday."

Zala smiled at her daughter's enthusiasm, a bittersweet ache tugging at her heart.

Zuri's innocent joy softened her guarded heart, reminding her of the simple things that made life feel normal. Zala leaned down, brushing a loose curl from Zuri's forehead. "I'm sure they do, sweetheart," she said. "We'll find a place that serves waffles just as good as the ones in New York."

Zuri nodded, satisfied with her mother's answer, though she didn't seem to fully grasp the weight of what Zala had just said. It wasn't just about the waffles for her; it was the routine, the feeling of home they had built in those moments.

But Zala couldn't help the sinking feeling in her chest. Zuri, her bright-eyed, innocent girl, had no idea that things were changing again in ways she couldn't control; she hadn't told Zala that they wouldn't be returning home to the big house in Addis Ababa.

"Maybe we can make it a tradition," Zuri added, eyes wide

with excitement. "Every weekend, we eat waffles mummy, just us."

Zala's heart twisted in her chest.

The weight of Zuri's words echoed louder than she wanted to admit.

Just us.

That had always been the plan. It had always been enough. But was it now? Could it still be enough with everything else she had to face? It had to be enough.

She nodded, gently squeezing her daughter's hand as if reassuring herself as much as Zuri, that things would be okay. "Just us, darling," she whispered, though her voice trembled slightly.

Zuri beamed at her.

Zala sighed. She wasn't sure what the future would bring, but she knew she couldn't let go of the love that held them together, her and Zuri and the memories of the past that lingered even as they moved into a new chapter.

A new chapter she hoped would be good for the both of them.

Zala pushed open the door to the café, the warm, inviting scent immediately enveloping her. The soft hum of conversation and the clink of cups and silverware added to the cozy atmosphere.

"Let's find out how nice the waffles here are," she said with a playful smile, already imagining the crispy, golden goodness of waffles she would order.

"Yippee!" Zuri squealed, her excitement bouncing through the air as she skipped ahead into the café, her little feet tapping on the tiled floor.

Her mother followed at a more leisurely pace, her eyes scanning the bustling café, before a waiter appeared and led them to an empty table by a window, where the soft afternoon sunlight filtered through.

Zala pulled out a chair for Zuri, who eagerly slid into her seat, her tiny hands smoothing the white napkin in front of her. Just as Zala was about to sit down, a voice sliced through the air, familiar and unmistakable, stopping her in her tracks.

Her heart skipped a beat.

"Zala."

She would know that voice anywhere, how could she not? They had once been very close.

Naade.

Why did she have to run into him here? The one place she thought she could escape, and yet fate seemed determined to work against her, as if to remind her of everything she had lost Tensing instinctively, she turned slowly, her stomach tightening.

There he was, standing behind her, that familiar, easy smile on his face.

"Naade, hi," she said, forcing a polite smile that didn't quite reach her eyes.

"Zala," Naade said, his voice carrying that polite, neutral tone that was at once too formal and not quite warm enough to erase the distance between them. There was a beat of silence before Naade added, "It's good to see you."

But then, as if to erase any awkwardness, he turned and gave Zuri a warm smile.

"Hey there, little one," he said, his voice light.

Zuri, who had been looking up at him with a curious expression, broke into a shy smile in return.

"Hello," she said softly, her wide eyes studying Naade intently. Zala couldn't help but smile at her daughter's expressions, which reminded her of how she had been as a young child. It was almost like watching a reflection of her younger self, the curiosity, the way she weighed people before fully trusting them.

Naade crouched down so he was eye level with her. "What's your name, young lady?"

"Zuri," her daughter replied, a bit more boldly this time.

"Zuri," Naade repeated, testing the name on his tongue. "Beautiful name. Do you like waffles?"

Zuri's eyes lit up at the mention of her favorite food, and Zala found herself feeling a twinge of surprise at Naade's ease with her daughter.

It wasn't just his charm; it was the way he made Zuri feel like she belonged in this moment. Like this was normal. But then, as if remembering herself, Zala cleared her throat softly, shifting her weight from one foot to the other, unwilling to let this brief moment of ease carry her too far.

"Yes, we came here for the waffles," she said, giving Naade a polite but careful smile. "Zuri and I were just about to eat."

"Sounds like a plan," Naade replied, standing back up, his eyes still on Zuri for a beat longer.

"How have you been, Zala?" Naade finally asked her.

"I'm fine. How have you all been?" she smiled politely at him.

"Oh, we are doing great." Naade replied, looking around the café before he turned to look at her again.

"I can tell; you guys looked amazing," Zala said, her smile bright but her eyes carrying a trace of something deeper. "It was good to see you all at Eko Hotel, even though you and Tseye ignored me. Given the circumstances, I can't blame you both."

Her voice was light, but there was an unmistakable sting behind her words, as if she was trying to brush it off but couldn't fully mask the hurt.

Naade's smile faltered for a brief second, a wave of guilt sweeping over him, then he shifted uncomfortably, looking away for a moment before meeting Zala's gaze again. "So, are you back in Nigeria for good?" he asked.

Zala almost sighed out loud as she wondered if she should lie, but what was the point? She was back here for good unless life took her somewhere else.

She took a deep breath. "I'm back in Nigeria. I needed a change of environment after my divorce, and I have always loved living here, you know that. I got a job here, so Zuri and I moved back here."

There, she had said it; getting it out in the open was better. She and Tseye had mutual friends and were bound to run into each other eventually.

Especially as they all lived on the island.

"Oh," was all Naade said, and Zala almost smiled.

She was sure he would call Tseye and tell him the news the moment he left her.

She smiled at the waiter standing a few feet away waiting to take her order and nodded towards Naade. "It was nice to see you again, Naade," she said, smiling at him as she turned to speak to the waiter.

"Well, I won't interrupt your lunch. Just wanted to say hi."

Naade said, nodding at her.

Zala felt an odd tightness in her chest. She had always found Naade's presence calming, but now, she wasn't sure how to react after everything that had happened between her and Tseye.

Zuri's innocent question broke through the tension like a soft breeze.

"Are you and mummy friends?" she asked, her gaze shifting back and forth between them, clearly curious.

"Yes, we are," Naade said softly, looking at Zala for a moment before turning back to grin at Zuri.

"Well, I'm glad we ran into you," Zala said, her voice steady now. "We'll catch up another time. I'm sure you've got your own plans."

Naade nodded, his smile softer now. "Take care of yourselves," he said, looking at Zala one last time before turning to leave. "I'll see you around."

Zala watched him walk away, her heart heavy.

When he was gone, she turned back to Zuri, who was already engrossed in picking out what she wanted to eat.

* * *

"I ran into Zala yesterday," Naade said as Eyimofe and Tseye looked over designs for their new lounge.

"What do you think of this design, guys?" asked Tseye, ignoring him.

"You heard Naade, didn't you?" Eyimofe asked, tossing the documents on the table before him.

Putting down the document he was holding, Tseye looked up at Eyimofe. "I heard him, why is he telling me? Why do I need to know?"

"Hey, I'm just making conversation," Naade continued his tone light but with an edge of playfulness, as he leaned back casually against the bar, drink in hand. He ignored the warning look Tseye was shooting his way. "I also met her delightful daughter," he added, a smirk tugging at the corner of his mouth as he sipped his drink.

"Naade…" Tseye began, his voice low.

Naade raised an eyebrow but didn't flinch. He had always been the more carefree one, the one who didn't hesitate to push boundaries when it came to his best friends. "What? I didn't say anything wrong," he replied, his eyes scanning Tseye's face for any sign of weakness.

He was used to reading Tseye, to seeing through his friend's tough exterior but right now, there was something in Tseye's eyes that stopped him short. It was a mix of frustration and… some- thing else.

Something Naade hadn't seen in a long time.

Pain.

"I'm glad you had a delightful time with her and her daughter; why do I need to know that?"

Naade shook his head slowly. "I am not trying to be funny or act like I don't know what she did to you." He paused. "I know you, Tseye, and one thing I know is you aren't over Zala Kebede."

Tseye got up, shaking his head, as he strode away from his friends.

"I don't know what you are talking about, and I don't need to know anything about Zala; why are we even speaking about her? Next, you will tell me about her husband."

"I was getting to that; she's divorced; imagine how happy I was to know that the man she left you for is no longer in the picture, karma, eh?" Naade leaned back in his seat, chuckling, as he looked from Eyimofe to Tseye, who shook his head in disbelief.

"How petty and childish can you be?!" Tseye hissed as Eyimofe burst into laughter.

"I agree, I am all that, but I felt happy knowing that she was divorced. As a friend who was by your side when you were heartbroken and sobbing, I was happy to know her marriage did not work out."

"I never cried, you moron!"

"You did!" Eyimofe smirked. "And any opportunity to drink, you were up for it. Do you know how many times

43

we had to carry you home drunk? You almost ruined my reputation, bro! And poor Misan almost broke her back from pulling you around your apartment."

Tseye, now scowling at his friends, threw his hands up in defeat. "How are we still friends?"

"We are brothers for life, I just felt you needed to know why she was back in town, seeing as you were curious," Naade explained calmly.

"Thank you for letting me know. I wonder what gave you the impression that I was curious about her. It's information I don't need. Now, can we get down to business?"

* * *

Tseye waited for his friends to leave before he poured himself a drink and downed it in one go.

Zala Kebede

The best and worst thing that had ever happened to him.

He still had the ring he had planned to propose with; the ring was tucked away in the desk in his study. He had decided not to return the ring but had kept it as a reminder of how stupid and trusting he had been.

He shook her head as he remembered how he had pleaded with her.

And then she delivered the final blow that had broken him

and shattered his trust in women. She was going back home because she was getting married.

How insensitive could a woman be?

They had been together for four years, and she had lived with him in the last two years of their relationship, so it had come as a shock to know that Zala had been planning to get married the whole time without telling him.

Her actions had ruined him for women, since then, Tseye had never been in any serious relationship.

Oh yes, he had dated a little, but nothing serious. He couldn't bring himself to trust any woman at all.

Now, she was back in Lagos with a daughter, and for the first time since she had left his life years ago, Tseye was worried that he still had feelings for her.

Chapter Four

"**D**o we still have Lola Edun's number?" Tseye asked as he strode into the small meeting room where his friends were having a quick breakfast before their meeting.

"Why would we still have Lola Edun's number, and why are you asking for it?" Naade asked as he looked from his plate loaded with eggs and bacon.

"Do we still have it?" Tseye repeated quietly.

"I do. She works with MTN, and I ran into her a few months ago," Eyimofe responded as he began going through his contact list on his phone to get the phone number Tseye was asking for. "Why do you need it, Tseye?"

Knowing he couldn't lie to his friends, Tseye took a deep breath and said calmly.

"I want to get Zala's number from her."

There was silence after his reply as his friends looked at him without saying a word.

Then Eyimofe said quietly, "I just sent her details to your phone; why do you need to speak to Zala?"

"Who knows, I may just want to catch up."

"You could have done that when you saw her in Eko Hotel the night of my party. You chose to walk away and ignore her when the mature thing to do would have been to say hi. Now you want to catch up with her? Are you nuts, man?" Naade dropped the cutlery he was holding to glare at Tseye.

Ignoring his friends, Tseye walked to the glass windows overlooking the busy road beneath it; his smooth fore-head creased in a frown as he mulled over what Naade had just said.

He had ignored her because seeing her caught him off guard. He would get Lola's number and call her when he had mustered enough courage to do so.

"What do you want to say to her?" Eyimofe murmured.

"I don't know, I just want to speak to her; I can't stop thinking about her," Tseye replied quietly.

"Tseye." Eyimofe said quietly, "She is fresh from a divorce, and from what Naade said, she came here to heal; a woman healing from a breakup needs time and space to heal."

"Huh?" Naade turned to look at Eyimofe, an incredulous look on his face. "Says the one who chased after Yahimba; tell me, wasn't Yahimba still healing from a breakup when you began pursuing her?"

"Shut up, Naade," Eyimofe snapped. "It's not the same, and you know it."

"Na true, how your own take different?" Naade chuckled, speaking in pidgin, ducking as Eyimofe threw a tissue at him. "Eyimofe is right, though, Tseye. Are you sure about that? Calling Zala?"

"I won't know until I do, but I just need to speak to her," he said, pausing and turning to face his friends. I know it's been over three years now but seeing her made me realize one thing: I may still have feelings for Zala, and I need to speak to her to put all this behind me once and for all."

"You want my advice?" Eyimofe asked.

"No, but you are going to give it anyway." Tseye said resigned.

"Stay away from her."

* * *

Zala's confident stride echoed softly against the polished marble floor as she walked through the sleek lobby of the MTN office building on Adetokunbo Ademola Street.

Her blue jeans fit her like a second skin, and her crisp white shirt accentuated her figure, giving her an effortlessly sophisticated yet casual look.

As she entered the lobby, it was impossible to ignore the effect she had on the room.

Heads turned, both male and female, drawn to her presence like moths to a flame. Zala was no stranger to the attention, but it never made her feel more aware of it. She simply moved through the crowd, unbothered, as though it was just another part of the world she navigated.

Ignoring the admiring looks, she pushed forward, focusing instead on the task at hand. Opening her purse, she pulled out her phone and quickly dialed Lola's number, tapping her foot lightly on the floor.

Her friend answered immediately.

"Where are you, Lola?" Zala's voice was steady, but there was an edge of impatience in it, the kind of tone that suggested she had a lot to do and wasn't in the mood to waste time.

Zala glanced around the bustling lobby, spotting a few familiar people. The building seemed to buzz around her, a steady hum of conversation and activity, but Zala barely noticed it.

This trip to the MTN office was more than a social visit. She had things to discuss with Lola, things that could change everything.

Lola's voice came through, cheerful and bright as always. "On my way down to you, saw you walk in from my office," her friend replied, sounding out of breath.

"Oh, okay, I will wait by the fountain."

Zala cut the call and, nodding at the receptionist, walked to the fountain by the tall windows and sat in the waiting area.

She was nervous.

She had asked Lola to get Tseye's number and office address.

Lola had been reluctant but had finally given in to her pleas, providing the information she had asked for. Now, she sat here in the lobby of MTN, waiting to see Lola before heading to Tseye's office. For the hundredth time, she wondered why she was going to see him and what she would say if he agreed to speak with her.

Lola asked the same question moments later as they walked to her car.

"What are you doing, Zala?" "I just want to see him, Lola."

"You already saw him at Eko Hotel, and he snubbed you. Do you think Tseye will hug you and ask how you've been? You broke him, left him and married someone else," Lola said firmly.

"I had no choice, Lola!"

"You did, but let's not argue about that. You chose to end your relationship and did not fight for what you both had; you got married, and now that you are divorced, you want to speak to Tseye? Please don't blame me for not supporting you, Zala, and I do not think it's a good idea."

"What is the right thing to do, Lola?"

"The right thing to do is stay away, keep your distance from Tseye."

"I can't, Lola."

"You can't, or you won't?"

Zala shook her head slowly, tears gathering in her eyes. "You know the reason, I can't. I also can't be in the same city, knowing he hates me; I want a chance to explain my actions. I'm not that stupid to think he would take me back."

"You've been here for six weeks and only seen him once; what makes you think you will run into him soon? You two don't move in the same circles anymore," Lola pointed out.

"I just have to do this; it's important."

"Oh, Zala," Lola whispered as she hugged her friend. "You are the last person Tseye would want to speak to, and I don't want you getting hurt; you've been through so much already, and I know you never got over Tseye, which is why I don't think this is a good idea."

"At least you will be here to hand me tissues when I return." Zala chuckled as she pulled back to look at Lola.

"You know I have your back, always," her friend replied.

* * *

"Zala just walked into the reception," Naade announced as he strode into Tseye's office.

"Zala, who?" asked Eyimofe, sitting at Tseye's desk and looking through documents as Tseye swung around to look at Naade, an incredulous look on his face.

"What are you talking about, Naade?"

Naade grinned at the reaction he was getting from Eyimofe and Tseye. His friends' confused expressions clearly indicated that they weren't quite following.

"I said, Zala just walked into our offices." Naade's voice was casual, but there was a certain knowing edge to it, like he was enjoying this moment more than he should. "You know Zala, right? The one you've been talking about for the past couple of days?" Naade continued leaning casually against the doorframe. He raised an eyebrow, his tone teasing, as he dropped the bombshell with a smirk. "The same Zala you've been avoiding for weeks, even though you have Lola's number, the number you asked for so you could get Zala's contact from her, but never did"

Eyimofe looked up from the stack of papers, a frown furrowing his brow as he glared at Naade. "Zala is here?" he asked, glancing back at Tseye, watching for his reaction.

Tseye's eyes narrowed, his expression shifting from disbelief to something much darker, something that felt almost like dread. He stood from behind his desk, his chair scraping loudly against the polished floor.

"Why would Zala be here?" he muttered.

"I asked them to direct her to your office while I came to get Eyimofe out so she can come in. You are telling me you are not curious?" Naade replied.

Tseye's hands clenched into fists, as he willed his heart to slow down.

"I am not, Naade," he said through gritted teeth. "She left, Naade. She walked out of my life, and I'm not sure how I'm supposed to feel about that."

Eyimofe studied Tseye for a moment before speaking, his voice quieter, more measured. "Tseye, we all know how you feel about her. We've known for a long time. But you are also avoiding the fact that you never got closure. And I think you are afraid of what might happen if she actually comes in here and talks to you."

Tseye's eyes darted to his best friend, and for a moment, a flicker of uncertainty passed through him.

He didn't want to admit it, but Eyimofe was right. There

was unfinished business between him and Zala, and to his dismay, his feelings for her had never really disappeared.

Even after all these years, a part of him still wanted answers.

Needed them.

Eyimofe finally spoke up, his tone more serious. "Tseye, you know you don't have to handle this alone. We are here for you. But if you want answers, you might have to face her."

Tseye paused, staring out the window as if contemplating something far deeper than the conversation at hand. His hands were shoved deep into his pockets, and he was silent for a long moment.

His friends were right though, if she was here, he couldn't avoid seeing her.

"Fine. I'll see her," he said quietly.

Naade and Eyimofe, nodded walking out of his office. Muttering a curse, he walked over to the glass windows, his gaze lingering on the chaotic scene below. Cars honked as pedestrians weaved through the crowded sidewalk, but none of it seemed to matter as his heart began to beat erratically.

What on earth was she doing here? And what did she want from him?

Chapter Five

Damn, he wasn't ready for this.

He didn't know if he could handle speaking to her.

He tensed as he heard his door open and knew she was the one who had just walked into his office.

Taking a deep breath, he turned around and immediately regretted listening to his friends.

He should have said he was in a meeting and asked them to turn her away.

The instant their eyes met, he knew he was in trouble as his heart slammed into his ribs.

"Hi, Tseye," she said softly.

And Tseye lost it; he had to stop himself from walking across to her, taking her in his arms and kissing her.

Instead, he looked away from her, forcing himself to control his emotions and how he felt.

"What are you doing here, Zala?" he asked, ignoring her greetings.

"I wanted to see you" she replied.

He turned to look at her, his mouth dropping open in surprise.

"What? What did you just say? Why would you want to see me"

"I said I wanted to see you, " she repeated, clenching her purse.

He noticed how tightly she held her purse.

A sign that she was nervous. Good, so she should be!

"You saw me in Eko hotel, didn't you?" he asked her.

"We didn't speak." She replied.

"I'm glad you remember that because, from my actions, it was clear that I didn't want to speak to you; let me repeat this, Zala, I never want to speak to you or see you as we have nothing to discuss."

Lies!

"Tseye, please."

"You shouldn't have come Zala; we have nothing to say to each other, Zala."

"Tseye, please listen to me." Her voice broke, her defenses

crumbling. "I just want to clear the air between us; please listen to me," she pleaded as their eyes met, hers pleading, his filled with disgust.

His gaze was dark with years of unresolved anger.

"Lis- ten to you? Why should I, Zala? You think you can waltz back into my life after everything and apologise for what? For breaking me? For abandoning me with no explanation? No, that's not how this works." He slammed his fists on his desk, "No, you no longer have that right to speak to me or be in the same space with me, so I'm going to ask you politely to leave my office."

* * *

Zala's eyes filled with tears, but she didn't back away.

She swallowed hard, the words barely finding their way out.

"I know I hurt you. I... I never meant to. It was a mistake. I should have told you why. I should have—"

"Why, Zala?" Tseye's voice was harsh now, the pain from four years ago spilling into the present, burning his heart all over again as he abandoned his decision to ignore her. "Why? Why did you walk away? What was it all for? Was I not enough? Was my love not enough?"

Zala's breath caught in her throat at the raw pain in his voice.

"No, Tseye, it wasn't that. I-" She stopped, her voice breaking. "Please," she said, voice shaky but earnest. "I know I don't deserve your forgiveness, but I need to explain. I need to tell you why I did what I did." Her hands trembled at her sides. "Tseye, I didn't walk away because I didn't love you. I didn't leave because I wanted to hurt you. I was terrified, Tseye. You have to understand that."

"I've heard enough," he snapped, turning his back to her, then he turned back to face her, his expression unreadable. "You cheated on me, or how else can you explain, getting married within three weeks of leaving me?"

"I didn't cheat on you, Tseye. Never."

"What? You got engaged within one week of breaking up with me!"

"I didn't cheat on you." She paused, then reached out to touch him, wincing when he stepped back from her. "I didn't cheat on you, Tseye; I lied as that was the only way I could get you to accept our breakup. I had to marry Negasi; it was a marriage to advance my father's political career."

"You had to do what?" Tseye shouted now, moving behind his desk so she stood on the other side of the table.

"You broke up with me for that?" He shook his head slowly as what she said sank in.

"Tseye?"

He looked up, and their eyes met.

"You need to leave now, Zala, while I am still calm and polite. You know it would have been better if you cheated on me; breaking up with me for that reason is worse, and I will never forgive you for that. We have both moved on, and that's good; now, please leave and stay the hell out of my life!"

He didn't wait to see if she would comply and leave but walked around his desk, past her and out of his office.

* * *

"We could hear shouting from over here," Naade remarked minutes later when Tseye walked into Eyimofe's office. "Are you okay?"

"I wanted to grab and kiss her when she entered my office. What does that make me? Pathetic, right?"

Eyimofe slowly shook his head. "No, it means you are human."

"Man." Tseye dropped his head in his hands. "She wanted to talk; she says she didn't cheat on me but had to marry Negasi, whatever his name, to advance her father's political career, that hurt more than the thought of her cheating."

"That's good that she didn't cheat on you then," Eyimofe said.

"What difference does that make? She broke up with him, didn't she?" asked Naade from where he was sitting.

"It makes a whole lot of difference; it's obvious that feelings are still there," explained Eyimofe.

"Are you nuts? Or has love or Yahimba made you soft in the head? Why on earth would he date Zala again?" Naade demanded." Eyimofe said.

"I didn't mention dating her, you did.

"Hey!" Tseye looked up at his two friends, who were discussing him as if he weren't in the room. "I'm still here," he said, pointing towards himself.

"Look at him, Naade; his first comment was he wanted to kiss her; how long do you think he will last before he goes after her again?" Eyimofe ignored Tseye and spoke to Naade.

"Good question," Naade replied as he and Eyimofe turned to look at Tseye.

"Are you both done discussing me like I'm not here?" he asked.

His friends nodded.

"Good, let's forget Zala and get back to work; Zala Kebede is history and will remain in the past where she is meant to be; the fact that I say I wanted to kiss her does not mean I would be foolish to have anything to do with her, so forget placing any bets on how long before I fall."

Chapter Six

Zala waited until Lola had hung up and then dropped her head in her hands.

What was she doing?

Why was she doing this to herself? Tseye had practically thrown her out of his office, yet here she was, planning to go to his apartment.

The truth was that she wasn't over him; she had never stopped loving him, and that had eventually destroyed her marriage, it was one of the reasons Negasi had never had a chance with her, that and his bullish ways.

It wasn't like her marriage had been perfect.

It had been the opposite, and she had the scars to prove it.

Tseye had made his feelings clear where she was concerned. Still, she had to see him and clear the air, or she would never be able to live with herself.

A tiny voice kept telling her this was a big mistake, but she was past caring.

Sighing, she got to her feet and headed towards the kitchen to find her mother, who was busy overseeing dinner preparations.

"Where is Zuri?" she asked.

Mariam Kebede looked up from the vegetables she was chopping and smiled.

"In the garden, reading a book, are you okay? You look stressed, Zala."

"I'm fine, Mum," her daughter replied, taking the knife from her mother and chopping the vegetables as her mother turned to speak to the cook, who was waiting for her instructions.

Zala waited until the elderly woman who had accompanied them from Ethiopia left the kitchen before she turned to her mother and said,

"Would it be okay to leave Zuri with you for a few hours? I'm meeting Lola for drinks."

"Oh, Lola, how is she? She hasn't come to see me since we got in."

"She's OK, Mum. She did say she would be spending the weekend with us so that you would have her all to yourself. I'm meeting her for drinks and then dinner," she lied again.

"That's fine; you need a breath of fresh air. You've been indoors since we arrived, and your father is beginning to worry for you."

"I'm fine, Mum," Zala insisted.

"Zala," her mother said quietly as she reached across, took the knife from her daughter and laid it on the table. She waited until her daughter turned to face her, then said quietly, "You've been tense since we left home. I know you are unwilling to speak about what happened with your ex, but I want you to know we are here for you."

Zala smiled at her mum, reaching out to pull her into a warm hug

"I am fine, Mum."

"It doesn't look like that, Zala. Apart from when you eat with us, you shut yourself in the room all day; Zuri is the only reason you smile." She reached up to touch the scar above her daughter's eye, her voice breaking as she said quietly, "I miss my vibrant daughter. I want her back."

Zala shook her head slowly as she hugged her mother. "Mum, I am fine. I am just trying to get my act together and put my life in order. That's all. Listen, we can go shopping tomorrow and then have dinner afterwards. What do you think? Just us, Zuri, you and I; what do you think?"

Her mother nodded. "I would love that."

"Good," Zala beamed, stepping back. "I am going to get ready to meet up with Lola."

* * *

Tseye tossed his keys on the kitchen counter, tugging at his shirt as he headed to his room to shower, get dressed and join Yahimba, Naade and Eyimofe at Sailors, Lekki. Since Zala had come to his office two days ago, he had been unable to get her out of his mind.

His dreams were filled with her; his thoughts were filled with memories of her.

Of what they'd had, of all the times he had held her in his arms.

He couldn't get her out of his mind, which drove him mad. Eyimofe may be right; it wouldn't be long before he gave in to his feelings and called her, but he was determined to fight these feelings. He was disgusted with himself for thinking of her, especially as she had thrown away all they had to marry Negasi.

He recalled seeing pictures of them on their wedding day and wondered what she had seen in the bullish-looking man in the picture. He had been at a loss as to why she had married him. Now, he knew why: to advance her father's political career.

Eyimofe had labelled them "Beauty and the Beast."

Cursing himself for letting his mind wander back to her, he stepped out of the shower, the steam still hanging in the air. He dried himself off with the towel, rubbing it over his skin, trying to shake off the thoughts that wouldn't leave him. Sliding into a pair of well-worn jeans, he reached for his phone just as it began to ring, the sharp sound cutting through the silence of the room.

He answered on the third ring. "Hello?"

"Hi, Tseye"

He knew her voice the moment he heard it, unmistakable, warm and soft, like a sound that had been imprinted on his soul. His breath caught in his throat, the familiar warmth of her tone sending a ripple of memories through him, each one more vivid than the last. It was as if time had slowed, and for a split second, nothing else mattered but the sound of her voice.

"Tseye, it's me, Zala," her voice trembled slightly, as if she was holding back something more. "I'm parked outside your house... Please, can I come up?"

The rawness in her voice shattered the last of his resolve. Just like that, his defenses crumbled, leaving him exposed and vulnerable.

His mind screamed at him to say no, that he had company, but his body was already moving before he could stop himself. Every instinct told him to refuse her request, but somehow, he knew he couldn't turn her away.

"I am on the tenth floor" he said cutting the call as.

He was waiting by the massive, ornate black doors that led to his penthouse apartment when the lift doors slid open. His breath hitched, as she stepped into view. For a moment, everything around him seemed to blur, the polished floors, the sleek walls of his luxury building, all of it faded as his focus sharpened on her.

The way she moved, the way she hesitated just for a second before meeting his eyes, sent a wave of emotions crashing over him. The years, the silence, the anger, the unresolved feeling came rushing back, overwhelming him in an instant. She wore a dark green shift dress with no make-up, just simple earrings, a necklace, and a wristwatch, and she looked as sexy as hell.

"Hi." She came to a stop before him.

"How did you get my address?" he asked without mincing words, aware that the mood around them had changed.

She didn't bother to lie. "Lola gave it to me."

"Lola, eh?" Tseye replied, remembering he had run into Lola a couple of months ago when she had attended a house party in the apartment beneath his own.

"Are you going to let me in?" she asked quietly.

He stepped back. "Since you are here, you might as well come in," he stated, moving back so she could walk into his apartment.

She nodded, swallowing hard, as he stepped aside to let her pass.

The first thing she noticed upon entering his apartment was the expansive floor-to-ceiling windows on the far side of the room, offering a breathtaking view of the city skyline. The apartment was a masterpiece, with a blend of contemporary elegance and vintage charm that gave it a timeless appeal. Soft, warm lighting illuminated sleek modern furniture, dark leather chairs paired with minimalist, polished wooden tables, while antique bookshelves filled with carefully curated collections added a touch of nostalgia. Plush rugs in rich hues softened the polished hardwood floors, and each piece of artwork seemed perfectly placed, contributing to the space's effortless sophistication.

She wasn't surprised by the exquisite décor; it was exactly the kind of refined taste she would expect from him Tseye had always exhibited impeccable taste.

She turned to face him as he closed the doors and swung around to look at her, his hands deep in the pocket of the kaftan he wore over jeans.

She said the first thing that came to her mind.

"Naade met my daughter and I, a couple of weeks ago before I came to your office," she blurted out. She immediately felt stupid when he looked at her like she had grown horns.

"At the flower shop? Yeah, he told me about it." "How's Eyimofe? He was with your lady friend at Eko Hotel the evening I ran into you guys," she stuttered, her words tumbling out in a rush.

She was acutely aware of how she was babbling, but the nerves clawing at her insides were too much to control. She could feel the heat of embarrassment rising to her cheeks as soon as the words left her mouth. Oh no, she thought. Why did I have to bring her up?

Her mind scrambled for a way to recover, but it was too late now.

"My what?" Tseye asked, his brow furrowing in confusion as he turned to her, his voice colder than she expected. The sharpness in his tone sent a small pang through her chest, and her breath hitched.

"The lady at Eko Hotel who was standing with you guys," she quickly clarified, her words feeling clumsy in the space between them. She winced inwardly as she said it, aware that she sounded jealous.

"Are you talking about Yahimba? That's my sister."

"Your sister?" she said, surprised. "I didn't know you had one."

"Me neither." He shrugged. "Long story."

"Oh," was all she said, looking away from him as his stare made her uneasy.

"What do you want, Zala? Why are you here? Because I know you didn't come here to talk about Yahimba."

"Tseye..." she began, but he stopped her.

"You have said all you want to say, and nothing else is left to say. Can you stop coming around me? You made your choice years ago, and I was okay with it." He paused. "Look, I'm not going to pretend and act like seeing you has not affected me; it has, and I can't stop thinking of you, but that's where it ends. You need to stop coming around me like this."

So, he was thinking of her? She felt a surge of emotion as she realised what his comment meant.

"I can't, Tseye." "What?"

"I can't stop trying to see you." She paused, then whispered, "I haven't been able to stop thinking of you since I ran into you at Eko Hotel."

* * *

Wait! What?

This wasn't how it was supposed to go. He was meant to tell her to leave, to keep away from him, to remind her that he was in a serious relationship. But her words and that passionate look in her eyes, they unraveled him.

He couldn't think. His heart was pounding in his chest, his thoughts spinning in a whirlwind of conflicting emotions as their gazes met and held. Before he could even process what he was doing, he moved towards her. He took one step, and then another and then he was standing before her, so close to her, he could hear her heart beating.

"What did you say?" he asked her.

"I said, I can't stop thinking about you Tseye" she said simply.

Her words hit him like a tidal wave, sending a shockwave through him, igniting feelings he thought he had buried long ago. And then, with no more hesitation, no second thoughts, he took a step forward, closing the distance between them. His body moved as if on its own, and before he could stop himself, his arms instinctively wrapped around her, pulling her into the warmth of his embrace.

Before either of them could say another word, his lips found hers.

It was a kiss that was anything but careful, anything but controlled. It was fierce, desperate, passionate, as though they were both trying to make up for lost time. His mind screamed at him to stop, to push her away and remember that she wasn't meant to be here with him, but in that moment, none of that mattered. It was just the two of them, their lips crashing together, kissing like their lives depended on it. He pulled her closer, shuddering when he felt the connection between them, that shocking pull. It was as though they became one, as though she melted into him, moaning as he kissed her.

When her hands slid up to curve around his neck, he pulled back to look at her, and their eyes met and held. Then he bent his head again and captured her lips in another searing kiss, pulling her closer as his hands settled on her waist, holding her close to him.

They kissed like they couldn't get enough of each other; Tseye felt his heart slam into his ribs as her mouth opened beneath his and her tongue mated with his, her tiny hands clutching his kaftan, her full breasts pressing against his chest. He felt himself harden as they kissed and kissed, not stopping to breathe; it had been years since a woman had turned him on like this.

Correction, no woman turned him on the way Zala did. "Zala," he muttered, breaking away but she held him close, kissing his chin. He closed his eyes and lifted her into his arms, looking down at her as her arms slid up around his neck.

He didn't look away from her as he walked her through his apartment and to his bedroom. It was dark when he walked in; not bothering to switch on the light, he walked across the thick carpet to his bed. Setting her down at the foot of his king-size bed, he kissed her again, pulling her closer as she clutched at his kaftan, kissing him back.

She tasted like magic.

And he couldn't get enough of her. A little voice told him to stop.

He tried to ignore it because stopping was the last thing on his mind. But he couldn't stop, not now, not with the way she was kissing him back, pushing close to him, and making him feel things he didn't want to feel.

But common sense prevailed.

Breaking the kiss, he pulled back regretfully, pushing her away.

"We have to stop Zala," he muttered, stepping back from her. However, she moved quickly back into his space.

"Tseye?" It was a question.

He shook his head slowly. "We have to stop, Zala; we can't do this?"

"I don't want to stop," she whispered.

"Why?" his voice was hoarse as he looked won at her.

Their eyes met and held, and he waited for her to speak. "Make love to me, Tseye," she whispered.

He didn't need to hear more because this was precisely what he needed and all he had been thinking of since she had come back into his life.

And so that was what he did.

He moved to her, pulling her into his arms, bending to kiss her as he guided her to his bed. He gave her precisely what she asked for. He made love to her over and over again.

Chapter Seven

It was still early when she woke up.

She glanced at the antique clock on the wall.

It was almost 6am.

Zala turned to look at Tseye, who was still fast asleep.

She didn't want him to wake up before she left. Last night was unexpected but worth it; despite how she felt, she didn't know how to face him if he woke up. She had come here for something else and ended up in his arms and bed.

It had felt right, yet so wrong.

Slipping on her shoes, she turned to leave the room and stopped when he spoke from behind her.

"So that's how it's going to be? You walk out on me after last night?" His voice was cold.

"I h-have to leave," she stammered. "Last night should never have happened, Tseye."

"You know that now? It didn't feel that way when you were in my arms last night, Zala!" he snapped.

"That's not a nice thing to say." Her voice quivered as she looked at him, her eyes pleading with him to say nothing. "Let's just forget it happened?"

"Really?" he remarked, sitting up in bed and folding his arms. "Am I supposed to forget that we spent most of the night making love? Or ignore the scars on your body, Zala?"

At the mention of her scars, her head snapped up. "Don't do this, okay? I came to speak to you but ended up in your bed. I admit I couldn't help myself, and yes, I still have feelings for you, but last night should never have happened, so I'd rather we forget it," She pleaded.

"Like hell, I will!" Tseye yelled, pushing himself out of the bed and stepping closer to her, his voice sharp with anger. "You walked out on me years ago, got married, got divorced, and then came back! The first chance you get, you jump back into my bed and now you're about to sneak out like what we did is sordid. Tell me, Zala, what part of me isn't allowed to feel offended by your actions?"

"It was a fucking mistake! I couldn't help myself! I never stopped loving you, and seeing you again just made me realize how much I had missed everything about you!" Zala shouted, finally losing control over her feelings. "Despite how I feel, this was not meant to happen. Can't you understand that? Please, Tseye, let me go."

"You must be the most selfish human being on earth; how I ever fell for you still confounds me! You only ever think of yourself, Zala!"

"That's not true; I came to talk to you; last night just happened; we couldn't help it!"

"For God's sake!" Tseye bellowed, slamming a fist on the table. "Why do you keep saying you came to talk to me? What is so important that you couldn't just say it and go?"

"I came to tell you that Zuri is your daughter!" Zala screamed back at him, her eyes filling with tears.

* * *

Tseye felt like the ground had been yanked from under his feet.

Zuri was his daughter.

The words echoed in his mind, looping over and over like a relentless mantra he couldn't shake.

"What?"

She had to be joking, right?

He closed his eyes, telling himself he had just imagined this conversation, but when he opened them, she was still standing before him, her eyes filled with tears.

"What did you just say?" he asked, as he want sure, he had heard right.

"Zuri, Zuri is your daughter. That's what I came to tell you, and why I have been trying to see you and it is also why I came back to Nigeria."

Tseye shook his head slowly.

When he spoke, his voice was so cold that she winced. "Are you saying that Zuri, the child you had with your ex-husband, is my child?"

"Yes." she whispered, her eyes filled with tears. "I'm sorry to spring this on you now."

"You are sorry?" He turned to face her. "What exactly are you sorry for? Ary you sorry for the fact that you got married knowing you were pregnant with my child? Make it make sense, Zala."

"I swear, Tseye, I didn't know. We only found out Zala wasn't his when she fell ill months ago and needed blood. His did not match, and so he had a DNA done."

"You weren't aware? So, you went straight from my bed to his, Zala?"

"Please, Tseye, let me explain," she pleaded, tears streaming down her face, unchecked. "Please, I had no idea; Zuri was not my ex-husband's child. I didn't even know I was pregnant with Zuri, when we broke up. I could never have kept that from you. The moment I found out, I started divorce proceedings and moved back to Nigeria."

Tseye stood staring at her as pain and hurt consumed him.

This was a woman he would have given everything to be with, moved mountains to be with, and yet she had hurt him again and again, but this was different.

She had been pregnant with his child and married that man.

He would never forgive her for this.

There was no escaping this. The past had come crashing into the present, and now, he had to deal with it. He had to figure out how to move forward, for his sanity, for his Zuri's sake.

Because, despite everything, she was his daughter. And that meant he couldn't walk away this time.

Not completely.

"Get out," he said quietly.

"Tseye?"

"Get out before I do or say something we will both regret; as for Zuri, my lawyers will contact you, and we will come to an agreement regarding her. When you feel up to it and are ready, I would love to meet her, but now I would be grateful if you leave my house! I am going to shower, and I don't want to see you here when I come out."

Muttering under his breath, he strode towards the bathroom, slamming the door after him.

She had left when he emerged from the shower minutes

later, toweling himself dry.

Pulling on a pair of shorts and a T-shirt, he walked out into the living room; he needed to leave the bedroom; he couldn't look at the bed without remembering last night and how out of control they had both been.

Right now, at this moment, he hated her.

* * *

Zala burst into tears when Lola opened her apartment door to let her in.

"Oh, babes," Lola said, hugging her as she pulled her into her apartment and took her straight to the living room.

"Is Leye around?" Zala asked, referring to Lola's husband.

"No, he is in Abuja, he's back tomorrow. I am guessing you told Tseye about Zuri?"

Zala nodded. "And?"

"He told me to get out."

"Are you surprised, Zala? You did that guy dirty." her friend remarked thoughtfully.

"Lola, you know I only found out about Zuri recently."

"Did you tell him that?" Lola insisted, wanting to know what Zala had told Tseye.

"I did."

"Oh, Zala! Tseye is a guy. You saying you had no idea that Zuri was his until recently would mean that you went from his bed straight to Negasi's bed or you were sleeping with both men at the same time."

"He said that."

"Do you know what that does to a guy? That must have hurt."

Zala shook her head slowly. "I'm so messed up, Lola; I couldn't even say anything when he asked about my scars."

"Your scars, how did he see your scars?" her friend asked, her eyes widening in shock when she saw the guilty look on Zala's face. "No, you didn't?"

Zala nodded sheepishly. "I did; I slept with him."

"Jesus Zala!" Lola snapped, getting to her feet. "What is wrong with you?"

"I couldn't help it, Lola!"

"So, what next? I am your friend, but I must be honest with you! What you did was stupid! Why would you sleep with Tseye knowing the history you guys have?" Lola demanded, exasperated. "I wish I could slap some sense into you!"

"It's because of that history I could sleep with him! Lola, please stop shouting! What am I going to do? I have told him about Zuri, and he said his lawyers will contact me."

"Lawyers ke?" Lola said, switching to pidgin English, a popular dialect in Nigeria. "Ah, wahala dey o! We will have to wait until they contact you to see what he wants. And where did you tell your mum you were last night?"

Zala had the sense to look shamefaced. "I told her I spent the night at yours."

"Ah, Zala, you owe me for this big time."

"After you advise me on how to sort out this mess with Tseye."

"What are you going to do?"

"I will give him a few hours and call him back."

Leaning back in her chair, Lola asked, "What did you tell him about the scars when he asked?"

Zala shook her head slowly as her eyes filled with pain. "Nothing; how do I tell my ex that I was a victim of domestic violence and the reason for the issues in my marriage was him? Negasi knew I only married him out of obligation and that I was in love with my ex. He always reminded me that every day of our marriage, he never failed to gloat over the fact that I wasn't with Tseye. What's worse, I paid the price for not loving him."

"Zala, you fought back and broke free, even if it came with a price. You are a strong woman; Negasi is and was the loser. Look how he cowered when you finally stood up to him." Lola clasped her hands. "And you were brave enough to face Tseye, knowing how he felt about you, but you need to make amends for the hurt you caused that guy."

"How do I do that?" Zala asked.

"Zala, he needs to get to know his daughter, not through lawyers; reach out and ask him to meet up with his daughter, let them know about each other without lawyers present."

"But Tseye said his lawyers would contact me?"

"That was hurt talking; you need to take the first step; I know what happened and what you've been through; he doesn't. You need to speak to him."

Zala smiled.

"I will; I don't have a choice, do I?"

* * *

He ended up going to Eyimofe's apartment with Naade, where they listened to Eyimofe moan about how Yahimba had reacted on seeing her ex-fiancé and sister at Sailors.

Tseye shook his head slowly.

"Give her a couple of days to cool off," he told Eyimofe, leaning back in his seat as he rubbed the back of his head.

"Are you okay?" Eyimofe asked, and Tseye nodded.

"Yeah, I was going to ask if you were okay. Tseye?"

Naade asked.

Was he? Tseye wasn't sure he was.

What would he tell his friends? he was still trying to process the fact that he had a child.

Sitting up, he said, " Not at all; Zala is driving me nuts.

I don't know what to do about her?"

"Zala? Zala Kebede?" Naade's incredulous tone had him wincing in shame; there was no way he could avoid telling them about his night with her.

His friends would roast him. Especially Eyimofe.

He almost laughed when Eyimofe turned to look at him as though he had grown two horns overnight.

"You can't be talking about Zala, Tseye. Did you meet up with her again after she came to the office? Are you nuts?" Eyimofe snapped. "I thought you were done with that chapter?"

Tseye closed his eyes and almost groaned aloud.

How could he be done with that chapter? Despite how disgusted he was with himself and angry with Zala, he couldn't stop thinking about her.

84

"We kind of have an arrangement that suits the both of us," he lied.

"Arrangement? What kind of stupid arrangement, Tseye? Do you remember what she did to you? Do you want to put yourself through that again?" Eyimofe demanded.

"No, I don't, but this time, I can't ignore her or act like she doesn't exist. I know what I am doing, guys," Tseye explained.

Did he?

He wasn't sure.

He turned as Naade muttered, "Well, it doesn't look like it; you've been out of it for the last couple of days. This was supposed to be a fun evening, but now it's ruined with issues with women. I didn't sign up to be an agony aunt, guys."

"No one asked you. Wait till you meet someone who has you wrapped around her finger like Yahimba has Eyimofe wrapped around hers!" Tseye retorted, feeling defensive; closing his eyes, he tuned out the banter between his friends and focused on the thought of his daughter.

His daughter, Zuri. What did she look like?

His daughter, he had a daughter, and he hadn't known of her existence till now; suddenly, he was angry again; how could Zala have done that to him?

He needed a drink, something strong to pull him out of his head, something that would drown out the noise and give him the chance to let loose, to party, and to forget about everything for a while.

He would call up Kene, the lady he had met at the bank weeks ago and ask her to meet them at Vertigo.

He looked up as Naade said, "I'm not the one who has an arrangement with his ex, am I?"

"Ouch, that hurt." He winced as Eyimofe and Naade burst into laughter. "Listen, guys, sitting here moping over women isn't doing any good."

"Speak for yourself, please. I am single and happy to be so, and I don't need the baggage that comes with women and relationships," Naade chuckled.

Tseye forced himself to smile, though he felt hollow inside.

"We understand, sir. Let me rephrase my statement: It's no good sitting here with Eyimofe and I moping over women. Let's hit the island. Vertigo is looking like a very good option now."

"Yeah, that's a good choice; Vertigo it is, then," Naade grinned.

Tseye waited for his friends to get to their feet before he said casually, "I spent the night with Zala; no, let me be blunt, more direct, so you don't start grilling me for details; I spent the entire night making love to my ex-girlfriend, she left my apartment this morning."

His comment had both his friends turning to face him, shocked.

"You what?" Naade spluttered.

Eyimofe's eyes widened. "Are you nuts, Tseye?"

"Well, I guess it was only a matter of time before that happened; I just hope you know what you are doing, Tseye," Naade said quietly.

"I do; she was in my bed all night. I have no regrets, so don't start with the lecture, Eyimofe," Tseye warned, "And that's not all."

"What else could have happened than the obvious?" Eyimofe asked.

"I am the father of her daughter, Zuri."

Chapter Eight

It was rare to see his friends express shock, especially Naade, who always had something snarky to say. Their comical looks almost made Tseye laugh out loud, but he didn't. Instead, he watched amused as Eyimofe dropped his keys on the center table and sat down; Naade followed suit, sitting down.

Both of them had their mouths open in shock.

"Did she know she was pregnant when she married that guy?" Eyimofe queried.

Tseye shook her head. "She says she didn't, that they only found out when Zuri fell ill and they needed blood. Her ex wasn't a match, so he had a DNA test done, and it came out that Zuri wasn't his child; that's what made her ask for a divorce and the reason she came back to Nigeria." His friends were quiet momentarily, and Naade asked,

"What will you do about it?"

"I don't know. I was shocked, and I asked her to get out."

"Why would you do that, Tseye?" Eyimofe said, shaking his head.

Tseye turned to look at him, surprised. "A moment ago, you were adamant that I have nothing to do with her; choose a side, Bro, and stay there."

"Hey, please understand me," Eyimofe said, his voice gentle but firm. "I don't want you to get involved with Zala, until you both figure out what you want from each other. But there's a child involved now, and that changes things." He paused, letting the words settle before continuing, his gaze steady and serious. "Whatever you might think of Zala Kebede, she must have had a reason for everything she did. If Zala had known she was carrying your child, she would've told you. You have to believe that."

"True." Naade nodded, agreeing with Eyimofe. "So, what are you going to do?"

"I'm not sure. My mum is going to go nuts. First, Yahimba, and now Zuri. She would say the men in our family are very active.," Tseye joked, trying to downplay the emotions he felt.

"Ouch! I wouldn't want to be a fly on the wall when you tell your mum."

"Me too. Interesting days ahead." Eyimofe nodded. "Ah,

women, what would we do without them?"

Tseye chuckled as Naade smirked at Eyimofe.

Leaning back, he closed his eyes as his thoughts returned to Zala. He had noticed the scars on her stomach and her back last night and wondered about it.

Had she been a victim of domestic violence? Because she hadn't had those when they had been together.

She had changed, too. The vibrant, confident Zala he once knew seemed to have faded, leaving behind a quiet, more reserved version of herself. The only time she had seemed to relax was when she was in his arms, the familiar warmth between them sparking fleeting moments where the old Zala would emerge but even then, there was a tension, a subtle wariness in her eyes, as if she feared offending him, as though some part of her still didn't feel safe with him.

What the hell had that devil done to her?

"I think Zala was abused by her ex. I saw the scars, but when I asked, she refused to speak about it."

"This just keeps getting worse; why are you still here, Tseye?" asked Eyimofe quietly. "We can hang out some other time; you know where you need to be."

"He's right, Tseye, a child is involved." Naade chirped in.

Tseye smiled gratefully.

They were right. He knew he had to deal with this, and he

would but the weight of it all had hit him like a wave. He needed time to process the overwhelming fact that he was a father. It wasn't just the shock of it; it was the sheer enormity of what that meant.

He wasn't ready for this, not yet.

"I will do right by my daughter; I just need time to process all this."

"Fair enough, just remember we are always here for you," Eyimofe said quietly.

"I know that, and I am grateful for that too."

****

"What are you going to do about Zuri and your parents?" Lola asked as they sat down for dinner at Circa Lagos. Her voice was calm, but there was an edge to it, a thread of concern woven into her words.

Zala's fingers tightened around the edge of the menu, the laminated paper crinkling under her grip. She forced herself to relax, inhaling deeply through her nose. She had been dreading this conversation, but she knew it was inevitable.

"I'm figuring it out, I don't know how to start the conversation." she said, her voice steadier than she felt. She didn't look up from the menu, pretending to consider the options even though the words had blurred into nothingness before her eyes.

Lola let out a quiet sigh, the kind that was heavy with unspoken thoughts. "You can't keep avoiding it. Zuri needs to know her father. And you need to tell your parents the truth."

A waiter appeared then, a polite smile on his face as he asked if they were ready to order. Zala was grateful for the interruption, nodding along to whatever Lola ordered for them both. It gave her a moment to collect herself, to build her walls back up.

When the waiter walked away, the conversation resumed, quieter now,

"Is Negasi still fighting for joint custody of your daughter, even after knowing that Zuri is not his child?" Lola asked quietly.

Zala nodded as she reached for a menu.

"That's messed up; how will you handle that?" Lola asked, her voice low but urgent as she leaned forward over the table. The dim lighting cast soft shadows across her face, but nothing could hide the worry etched into her features.

Zala looked up at her friend, her expression a mask of calm that did nothing to conceal the storm brewing behind her eyes. She folded her hands in her lap to keep them from trembling.

"There is nothing to say," she replied, her tone steady, almost too steady. "And I have no intention of letting my daughter anywhere near him. After the abuse I suffered at his hands, I would be stupid to allow Zuri near him."

Lola sighed as she looked around the restaurant. "Negasi is a monster, and I am glad you have left Addis Ababa. I'm glad you are back here in Nigeria too. I missed hanging out with you, you know."

"I should never have left."

"Zala? Do your in-laws know about Zuri?" her friend asked.

Zala looked up from the menu and smiled wryly. "Negasi was too ashamed when he found out Zuri was not his daughter. I will have to tell them about Zuri, when I have spoken to my parents." she paused and then said quietly, "If I had known I was pregnant, I would never have gotten married to Negasi."

"Speaking of Tseye, have you spoken to him since you told him?"

Zala shook her head as her thoughts drifted to Tseye. "He hasn't called."

"Are you going to call him Zala?"

"I don't know; I'm scared of his reaction, Lola. I didn't know what to expect; he was so angry. I think he was more furious about my relationship with Negasi, and he thinks I went from his bed straight to Negasi's bed."

"Didn't you?"

"That wasn't how it happened, Lola, and you know that."

"I know that, but he doesn't know that. Zala, if you hadn't found out about Zuri, would you have divorced Negasi?"

At her question, Zala looked away, a sad look on her face. "I tried to make it work, but I couldn't bring myself to love him; I just couldn't. He knew that, and that caused a lot of issues in our marriage; Negasi was also a victim like I was, stuck in a marriage with a woman who was in love with someone else."

"Don't do that. Don't justify all the things he did to you. Negasi was and is a horrible person, and you were stuck in a marriage with an abusive man, a very abusive one too and now he wants access to Zuri!"

"He will never get it; I wanted to get Zuri out of Addis Ababa first, then I would face him in courts. I am ready to expose Zuri's paternity if he insists, and he wouldn't want that, the shame will kill him!" Zala snapped, anger filling her as she thought of her ex-husband.

God, she hated him so much.

"If Tseye doesn't call by tomorrow, I will call him and ask if we can meet up."

"Atta girl, it's time you start living, and the first step is sorting out Zuri and Tseye."

"You are right; I have to do this."

She didn't have to wait till the next day. Tseye called her as soon as she got home.

"Can we meet?" he asked, straight to the point, his voice devoid of emotion.

"Yes, we can. I was going to call you. When do you want to meet?" she asked. If he could be cold and calm, so could she.

"I am somewhere in Ikoyi; I can send my driver to get you if that's okay?" Tseye hesitated. "Zuri?"

"She's in Abuja with my parents; she's back next week," she explained. "Listen, just let me know the address where you are, and I can make my way over there."

"Why? You don't want me to know where you are staying?"

Sighing, she murmured, "That's not it; I just don't want to cause you any inconvenience, Tseye."

"It's not inconvenient, Zala; text me your address, and my driver will pick you up."

* * *

He saw her immediately she walked in, his heart pounded so fast that he was sure the person sitting at the next table could hear it because he could hear it.

95

"Hey," he said, getting to his feet as she approached. The first thing he noticed was how nervous she was. Immediately, he remembered the scars on her back and stomach and the scar above her right eye, and he flushed with anger again.

What the hell did that bastard do to Zala?

"Thanks for calling, Tseye." She smiled as he pulled out a seat for her.

"You left me no choice, Zala," Tseye said wryly as he took the seat opposite her. "What did you expect? That I would stay away after you tell me that the child you had with your husband is my child?"

Zala winced at his tone. "Ex-husband," she whispered.

"Whatever." Tseye dismissed her last comment, trying to stay calm. "Why did you do it, Zala?"

He watched as she looked away, then turned back to face him, though she avoided eye contact.

"I didn't know Zuri was yours. I had no idea, Tseye, or I would never have married him."

Tseye said nothing as he watched her, then asked quietly, "Were you cheating on me back then, Zala?"

Her head shot up, their eyes clashing as her mouth dropped open in horror; "No! I never cheated on you; I would never have Tseye; you have to believe me!"

"Then why did you do it?"

Zala swallowed painfully as she looked away.

Why wouldn't she look at him? He wanted her to look at him when she answered his question. Leaning forward, he placed his arms on the table between them and repeated his question, "Why did you end our relationship, Zala?"

"I thought you asked me over because you wanted to know about Zuri?" she whispered.

"I will get to that, but first, we must discuss this. I can't have a cordial relationship with you if we don't get past this, and we have to because of Zuri."

"I know you resent me, Tseye" " she began, but Tseye cut her off.

"You are damn right I do, Zala, you walked out on our relationship; that's fine. That was your decision, and I was okay with it. Then you showed up and got back into my bed, and the following day, you tried to sneak out of my apartment; when I confronted you, you told me I'm a father, the father of your child! Christ Zala, you know how to kill a man's confidence."

"I'm sorry, okay! I messed up! And I am so sorry!" Zala burst out, turning to look at him, her eyes bright with unshed tears. "I'm sorry."

* * *

"I'm sorry," Zala repeated, pleading with him to understand. "I had no choice, Tseye."

She looked down at her hands as she blinked hard to prevent the tears from falling over; she couldn't cry, not now, not in front of Tseye.

She had done a lot of crying in her marriage, no more crying, she told herself.

"I had no choice; it was for my family. My marriage to Negasi was good for both families; my father got the career he had always wanted, and Negasi's father got the funds he needed for his family business."

"Was it a win for you, Zala? So, you gave up on us for that? For your dad's diplomatic career?"

"You would have done the same, Tseye," Zala retorted, frowning at him. "You would have done the same for your parents."

"Zala, that is the difference between us." I would never have given up on us, and my parents would never have made me choose," said Tseye softly.

"I know there is nothing I can say that can make you believe how sorry I am and how I regret my actions years ago," Zala explained.

"Why did you come to my house that night?" he asked, suddenly changing the topic, which surprised her.

"What?" she looked up, her eyes clashing with his. She almost immediately wished she hadn't looked up. Tseye had beautiful eyes.

"Zala, why did you come to my house that night?" he repeated quietly.

"I wanted to talk to you." She paused. "I wanted to see you; I miss you, Tseye."

Chapter Nine

His heart slammed into his ribs, but he forced himself to keep a straight face.

He was here to talk about Zuri, not about what had happened between them in the past, but he couldn't get the night she had spent in his arms out of his head. It was just lust, he told himself, but a voice inside his head told him to stop lying to himself.

He didn't know if it was love he felt for her, but he knew he still had feelings for her.

And he wanted her back in his arms.

Taking a deep breath, he closed his eyes, willing himself to be calm.

He thought of the calming exercises Yahimba had taught him a couple of weeks ago.

"When you feel stressed, close your eyes and count to ten, and you will feel much better".

He did that now, smiling inwardly as he thought of his sister.

"Zala?"

"Yes?" She looked at him.

"Tell me about Zuri?" he said, and he almost fell out of his seat when she smiled.

The smile transformed her face, and the corners of her mouth lifted as her eyes filled with joy and peace.

"She's delightful; you will love her, Tseye!" She picked up her phone to flick through pictures of her daughter stored on her phone.

"Here." She looked up as she reached across to pass her phone to Tseye, who took it from her and began to flick through the images she had on her screen. "She's almost four, very energetic."

Tseye felt a wave of emotions engulf him as he flicked through the images of his daughter.

Zuri.

He had a daughter; he was a father.

He smiled at the different images of Zuri laughing with her mother, her grandparents, and her Aunty Lola.

There was none of her with Negasi.

As though she could read his mind, she muttered, "I deleted all her pictures with Negasi."

"Why?" he asked before he could stop himself.

"He is not her father, and I am glad for that! I don't want any reminder of him in her life," she snapped angrily.

"I'm sorry I asked," Tseye offered quietly.

"No, don't be. It was an innocent question."

"Zala," Tseye said, leaning forward. "We have unfinished business, and I don't want it to affect Zuri. I am ready to wait to meet her when you feel the time is right, so please don't feel like I'm putting you under pressure."

"I want you to meet her now, Tseye."

"Are you sure?"

"Yes, she is in Abuja with my parents and will be back at the weekend. We can arrange an outing. Would that be okay?

"I would love that. Thank you, Zala." Tseye grinned and was rewarded with a bright smile.

He had a problem, though.

How was he going to break the news to his mother?

His father, he could handle; his mother was another matter altogether.

How on earth would he break the news to her and tell her that, like his father, he had a child?

* * *

Zala walked into the head office of ZTN Group on Awolowo Road with a smile on her face. Today was her first day at work, and she looked forward to resuming her duties. After her marriage to Negasi, she had stopped working and become a full-time housewife, something Negasi had insisted on.

Looking back now, she realised that he'd insisted on many things, imposed his overbearing rule over her, and she had just gone along with everything.

It had taken a lot for her to confront Negasi and leave her marriage. To her surprise, her friends back home were surprised and criticized her for leaving. She had lost count of the times she had been told she would regret it, and Negasi was a dream catch worth fighting for.

Dream catch indeed, she snorted under her breath.

She let him rule over her, controlling every aspect of her life, including what she wore, and she was glad she had come to her senses and made the right decision for herself and Zuri.

Thinking of Zuri, she frowned.

Her ex-husband wouldn't give up the fight for custody, a battle that irked her to no end. Zuri wasn't even his daughter, but he still insisted on claiming fatherhood, pushing forward with his plans to drag her through court. To make matters worse, his sister had called her earlier that morning, hurling insults at her about keeping Zuri away from her family. Zala had nearly screamed at her, barely holding herself back from snapping that Zuri was not his child.

Cursing under her breath, Zala stood impatiently, her fingers tapping against the cool surface of the reception desk as she waited her turn.

The receptionist was dealing with the people ahead of her, their voices rising and falling in the background. When it was finally her turn, Zala didn't need to say a word.

The pleasant-looking receptionist greeted her with a warm smile, already aware of who she was.

"Your team is waiting for you," the receptionist said. Zala gave a tight smile in return and nodded.

She followed the receptionist's directions, making her way toward the lift that would take her to the third floor.

* * *

Tseye walked into Shiro, his eyes scanning the bustling restaurant, searching for Eyimofe, who was meeting him for dinner. The ambient noise of clinking glasses and low conversations filled the air, but his focus remained on the crowd. Just as he was about to turn and ask the restaurant manager, a friend of his, for help, he caught sight of Eyimofe at the back, waving him over with a grin, clearly already settled in and waiting.

Nodding at the waiter beside him, he walked towards Eyimofe and sat opposite him.

"Have you ordered yet?" he asked. Shiro was packed full as usual.

"And good evening to you too!" Eyimofe shook his head.

Tseye smirked. "Why are you so irritable this evening? Yahimba running rings around you?"

"I wish! By the way, Naade called to cancel. He won't be joining us," Eyimofe chuckled. "He and his folks are having a meeting with Obehi and her parents; Naade is pissed, man!"

"That's good! About time someone rattled his cage," Tseye laughed. "What do you think of Obehi?"

Eyimofe shrugged. "She's gorgeous, hard-working and fun. And yes, she parties hard; Naade doesn't like that; he wants a quiet, unassuming wife. Obehi is the opposite, but seriously, Tseye, this is insane; who arranges their children's marriages these days?"

"Zala's parents did," Tseye replied quietly.

"Oh wow, you spoke to her about it?"

"Two days ago, we didn't speak much because she was

getting emotional, so I just stepped back."

"So, what are you going to do? About Zuri?" his friend asked quietly.

"I'm meeting her this weekend. Taking small steps, get to know her, and then tell my parents. I'm not looking forward to telling my mother; she is still recovering from the fact that my father has a daughter, and that daughter is dating her best friend's son."

"Wow, man, I feel for you, but look, you have a child, and that's beautiful; you should celebrate it."

"I know, but it's all too much right now, especially with Zala involved. I find myself thinking about her all the time, and that's not what I want; she's someone I can't be in a relationship with because I can't trust her not to take off again." There, he had said it, and it felt good to talk to someone. "I shouldn't have slept with her again."

"Yeah, that was a stupid move. You should at least have waited to see if co-parenting would work before sleeping with your child's mother. So, what if you meet someone you like Tseye?"

"I will move on. Zala and I are not in a relationship, so that should not be an issue."

"Really? After you slept with her?" Eyimofe asked.

"She was about to leave when I woke up; what does that tell you?"

"Zala is fresh from a divorce; mind you, I am not on her side; I'm on yours, but she's vulnerable at the moment, and you did say you believe there was abuse in her marriage, so what the hell were you doing getting her into your bed?"

"I didn't seduce her or get her into my bed like you suggest. It just happened, you moron, like you would act any different if it were you!"

"Tseye, I'm just saying you need to be careful. A child is involved now, and you both have a lot of history. It wouldn't be wise to start something with Zala if you are not going to be serious about her," his friend advised.

Tseye snorted, shaking his head.

"That's the problem. I've decided I want a chance at another relationship with her, and I am wondering what to do and how to convince her that we can try again." He paused, looking at Eyimofe, who looked at him like he had grown a second head. "What? You have no comeback for that? Did I shock you?"

Eyimofe shook his head, a look of disbelief on his face. "You are mad," was all he said before nodding at the waiter. "You are mad," he repeated as Tseye burst out laughing. "What's funny?"

"You!" Tseye chuckled, wiping tears from his eyes. "You look so outraged; come on, Eyimofe, you know me."

"Do I? A few weeks ago, you couldn't stand the sight of her or allow us to talk about her; now you are thinking of a relationship with her; are you sure you want to do this with Zala again?"

Tseye sighed, rubbing his forehead as he thought it over. Was he ready for another relationship with Zala?

He didn't know. Would it work? He didn't know.

He said as much to Eyimofe.

"Will it work? I don't know till I make a move."

Eyimofe nodded, then said quietly, "Whatever you decide to do, I've got your back, Naade, too; now, can we order food?"

"Yes, we can; I'm famished." Tseye grinned, sitting up.

* * *

Zala had just walked into the kitchen when her phone rang.

Glancing down, she frowned when she saw it was a number she didn't recognize.

An Addis Ababa number.

"Hello?" she said answering the call.

"Good evening, Mrs. Abeba," a strange voice answered her greeting.

"It's Ms. Kebede, thank you, and who is this, please?" Zala snapped not bothering to be polite, anyone addressing her by her married name was definitely from her ex.

"My apologies, Miss Kebede, your married name is still on documents with our office. My name is Aida Bekele, and I'm a legal assistant with your ex-husband's Legal team. I was asked to call and speak to you regarding the date set by the Family court. As you know, Mr. Negasi is requesting shared custody of Zuri."

Zala saw red.

"I received notice of his intent from his lawyer, and I believe my lawyer communicated to his legal team that there would be no shared custody of my daughter Zuri, and I will not be coming to Addis Ababa for any court hearing," she explained.

"I don't think you understand, Ms. Kebede. Mr. Abeba has the right to demand shared custody of his child with you, which he has done; we hope you will try to attend the court hearing, which is the reason for this call to confirm your attendance."

Zala closed her eyes as she swore under her breath.

Taking a deep breath, she said slowly, "There will be no court hearing, nor will there be any shared custody. I do not want to deal with my ex again, so please kindly inform him that Zuri is my child. I am sure he will understand my message." She paused, then said, "Thank you for your call.

Have a good day."

Then she cut the call, swearing out loud.

"How dare he?" she screamed. "After all he put me through? How dare he do this?"

And then she burst into tears

Chapter Ten

"Zala."

Zala looked up as the office assistant walked into her office.

"Mr. Tseye is here; you asked me to inform you when he gets here; he's waiting in the lounge downstairs."

"Thank you for letting me know." Zala smiled. Getting to her feet, she began gathering her things.

She had an hour before work closed, and since she hadn't had lunch, she was getting off work early. Tseye had called asking her out for drinks, and she had accepted instantly, telling herself they had to be cordial because of Zuri.

But that was a lie.

She wanted to see Tseye.

It had been a struggle, keeping herself from calling him over the weekend. Zala's mind had been spinning with everything that had happened: her confrontation with Tseye, the pain she had seen in his eyes when she had told him about Zuri.

And yet, she knew there was nothing she could do to fix the hurt she had caused him.

Thank goodness he had called her first, so it wouldn't be like she was eager to see him.

Tseye was standing by the reception, flicking through his phone, when she emerged from the lift.

For a moment, she stopped and studied him.

Tseye Harriman.

Of all his friends, he was the gentleman. Tall and handsome, Tseye caused eyes to follow him whenever he walked into a place. She could see a group of women in the corner, studying him and trying hard not to show they were checking him out.

She almost laughed as she resumed walking towards him.

Tseye Harriman oozed charm, class and wealth.

He turned as she neared him, and his eyes, a unique shade of brown, lit up as he smiled.

And Zala felt her breath catch.

"Hey." He smiled when she stopped before him. "You good?"

"I'm fine, and you?" she asked, falling into step beside him.

"I'm fine and hungry; I hope you are too," he responded as he waited for her to precede him before he followed her.

"I am; I didn't have lunch." She smiled at him; glad he wasn't uptight like he had been the last time they had spoken. She was beginning to see glimpses of the old Tseye, which relaxed her.

Despite what had happened between them recently, she knew it would be hard for anything to happen between them.

She wished, though, that something would, but that was a tall dream.

She would settle for an amicable friendship, though, because of Zuri.

"So, what do you want to eat? Steak? I know you love steak; we could go to Vici, the steak there is very good," he said casually.

"Oh yes! I would give anything to eat steak." Zala smiled.

"Vici it is then."

* * *

He hadn't had so much fun in a long time with a date. Sitting here with Zala reminded him of all the fun they'd had in the past and how easy it was to chat with her. She wasn't as lively as she had been, she was more reserved, but maybe marriage did that to women?

Did it? He wouldn't know, as he had never been married.

"Tseye?" she said, breaking into his confused thoughts.

"Sorry, did you say something? I got lost in my thoughts," he explained.

She cocked her head to one side and smiled. "What were you thinking about?"

He didn't mince his words. "I was thinking of you and how I would like to date you again."

He watched her eyes widen in shock.

"Zala?" he asked.

"I don't know what to say, Tseye. Everything that's happening between us again is so sudden, and you haven't even met Zuri yet," she whispered, looking back at him.

"Zala, I just said that. I'm not asking for an answer; I just wanted you to know how I felt, okay? You asked what was on my mind."

She said nothing, looking down as she worked her bottom lip with her teeth.

Reaching across, he took hold of her chin and tilted her face up so he could look directly at her. "Relax, Zala. I don't bite, okay? We came here to eat, and we will eat, and then

I will take you home like the perfect gentleman my mother raised me to be. If you want to hang out anytime, please call me, but for now, I need you to relax, okay?"

She nodded jerkily as she reached up to rub the scar above her eye.

Without thinking, he asked, "How did you get that scar?"

"I walked into a door," she mumbled. Pulling away from his hold, she blinked in surprise as he reached out and traced her scar with his finger.

Then, almost immediately, he pulled back, the corner of his mouth lifting in a wry smile.

"Let's eat, Zala, before I do something that will send you running in the opposite direction."

* * *

She took a cold shower the moment she got home.

After she had settled down, she reached for her phone and called Lola.

"Tseye wants a relationship," she said.

"Of course he would; you are the mother of his child," Lola grumbled.

"Why are you so grumpy?"

"Are you serious? Do you know what time it is? It's past

11 pm," Lola snapped at her, irritated.

"Okay, I'm sorry for waking you up, but I had to tell you he wants a relationship, Lola and not the kind of relationship, you think!"

"Eh?" Lola's voice changed, and Zala smiled as she could imagine her friend sitting up in anticipation of her gist. "What kind of relationship are you talking about?"

"Oh, so you do not want to sleep any longer?" Zala teased, laughing.

Lola's voice came through the phone, a mix of amusement and disbelief. "You better tell me everything, from start to finish. You've just succeeded in waking me up," she said, her tone light but clearly intrigued. Zala couldn't help but laugh, the sound a brief escape from the weight of her day.

"Date, he wants us to try again."

"What? Tell me you are kidding, Zala, after everything you did to him," Lola asked.

"I was shocked, too, Lola."

"What did you say?" her friend asked.

"What did you expect me to say? He caught me off guard, and just as I was getting myself together to respond, he changed the topic. Tell me, what was I supposed to say?"

"Oh wow."

"Is that all you have to say about it?"

"What do you want me to say? What do you want to do?" Lola asked again.

Zala was quiet for a while, then quietly said, "I don't know. I don't think I can have relationships again. And what do I do if I start something with Tseye and he wants something permanent like marriage?"

"Zala, Tseye is not Negasi. I am not asking you to date your ex," her friend pointed out.

"So, what are you saying?"

"I am saying you have been through a lot and deserve happiness. Don't let the experience of your marriage ruin relationships for you; it doesn't have to be Tseye; it could be anyone; you need to give whoever it is a chance, give yourself a chance to be happy; you deserve all the happiness you can get."

"I know that, Lola; I'm just scared."

"I know you are." Lola paused. "Listen, don't rush into anything; you just got back to Lagos, settle into your new job, get Zuri settled in school, get her to meet Tseye and his parents, take your time and then when you are ready, just do what's right for you."

Zala smiled at her friend's advice. "Thank you, Lola."

* * *

Zala was nervous. Zuri and her mum had arrived back from Abuja, a couple of minutes ago and were in the living room chatting.

She was nervous because Tseye was on his way here to meet Zuri.

Her parents had known of Tseye back then, and her mother would want to know why Tseye was here to meet Zuri. Sighing, she ran a hand across her forehead and almost groaned loudly when she felt the beads of sweat on it. This had to be done soon, so she might as well get on with it.

She was about to join her daughter and mother in the living room when the doorbell rang, its sharp tone cutting through the quiet.

Tseye was here.

Taking a deep breath, she reach for the door handle and pulled the open to see Tseye standing there, hands in the pocket of his well-tailored pants.

"If there's one thing about you that hasn't changed, it's your fashion style," she teased, a playful smile tugging at her lips as she opened the door to let him in.

He chuckled, the sound warm and familiar, as he walked inside. He paused for a moment, waiting for her to close the door behind him, before he said with a smile; "A man has to always look smart."

"Yeah, right," she grinned as she led him to the living room. "Zuri is in the living room; my mother is there. I haven't told her about you, nor have I said anything to Zuri. Is it okay if we say nothing when you meet them both?"

Tseye nodded as she pushed the glass doors to the sitting room, and he followed her in.

Her mother looked up from the book she was reading with Zuri, when she walked in, Tseye behind her.

"Hey, Mummy, do you remember my friend Tseye?" Zala asked.

Zuri got up immediately, squinting, her forehead creasing as Tseye stopped beside her mother.

"Good afternoon, Ma," Tseye said as Mrs. Mariam Kebede straightened up in her seat, her eyes, like those of her daughters, lit up with a welcoming smile.

"Of course I remember him. Tseye, it's been a while; how have you been?"

"I've been fine, Ma, and you?"

"Fine, as you can see, we are back in Nigeria."

Zala looked at her mother from the corner of her eye, knowing she was in for a grilling session when Tseye left. Her mother was her usual charming and friendly self, but she could see the wheels turning around in her head.

Ignoring her mother's questioning look, she turned to smile brightly at Zuri, who had come to Tseye and was smiling at him.

"Good afternoon," she said, smiling shyly at Tseye and introducing herself. "I am Zuri."

Tseye crouched before her as he returned her smile. "Zuri, I have heard so much about you?"

"Have you?!" Zuri squealed, her voice full of pure excitement as she touched his hand. "Mummy is always talking about me!" she continued, her words tumbling out in a rush, a bright grin spreading across her face as her eyes shone with joy.

"Yes, she is; I know a lot about you," Tseye teased.

Watching them, Zala realised, with a jolt, that Zuri looked exactly like Tseye.

Seeing them side by side now, it was apparent they had the same features, except for the eyes. Her daughter had inherited her dark brown eyes.

She was aware that her mother had turned away from Tseye and Zuri, who were conversing like old friends, to look at her.

As she did, her mother could see the resemblance between Tseye and Zuri.

She felt her mother's gaze burn into the back of her head.

She could feel the weight of that stare, even though she refused to turn around to look at her mother.

She couldn't. Not yet.

She and her mother would have that talk after Tseye left.

* * *

Tseye couldn't help but feel the warmth that washed over him when he walked into the living room and saw Zuri.

His daughter, he realised with pride, looked very much like him.

"I like you," his daughter said, hopping from one foot to the other, and he laughed as she winked at him.

Zala was right.

Zuri was delightful.

Well, she had to be. After all, she was his daughter, and she had his genes.

He looked up as Zala said something. "What?"

"I asked if you and Zuri would like to sit in the garden while I get some refreshments for you?'

"Oh yes, please. I would like that," he replied, getting to his feet as Zuri reached for his hand and smiled at him. He smiled and then added, "My new friend would want a drink, too."

"Yes! Orange juice!" Zuri squealed as they followed her mum out to the garden.

He ended up staying for dinner.

He noticed that Zala was a different person when she was around her daughter; she glowed, smiled, and laughed, and he could see that Zuri adored her mother and grandmother, too.

A wave of warmth washed over him as he imagined introducing Zuri to his parents. She was a delight to be with, and he knew she would captivate them instantly with her mischievous smile and toothless grin, her infectious energy winning them over just as it had with him.

He couldn't wait for his parents to meet his daughter. He couldn't wait for her to meet Eyimofe, Naade and

Yahimba too.

* * *

"Thank you for letting me meet her," he said two hours later as they stood by his car.

"I am glad you did. She already likes you. I still have to tell her you are father, though."

"Small steps, Zala." He paused, then said quietly. "She speaks well for her age."

"I know. My mum said I spoke at two." She chuckled. "Did

you drive yourself?"

Tseye looked down at his wrist as he winced. "I had my driver, Akin drive me over, as I hurt my wrist, but he had to leave as he had a prior engagement. I should be able to drive home. My house isn't far from here."

Zala nodded. "Thank you for coming, Tseye," Tseye nodded as their eyes met.

"So, when can I come over again for a visit and how will you explain my coming here today to your mother?"

"I'm not looking forward to it, trust me," Zala grumbled with a heavy sigh. "But she won't let it go."

"I don't envy you at all," he laughed. "You might as well go all in, so you don't have to explain twice," he added, suddenly moving and reaching for her, chuckling as she looked up at him in surprise just before he bent and kissed her.

He had been waiting to do that all evening, he realised as she gave in to his pressure to kiss him back, her small hands clutching his shirt.

Only Zala could make him feel like this just by kissing him; how could he have forgotten how it felt to kiss her?

She touched his cheek, and it lit a flame in him, which seemed to light one in her as he felt her shudder when he reached down and held her hips, pulling her hard against him.

He was losing it; he had to stop, he told himself.

Forcing himself to stop kissing her, he whispered against her mouth, "Zala, I can't stop thinking about you, and I can't deny the fact that I want to take this further."

"I want it to, Tseye, but it's too soon."

"No, it's not," he groaned, pressing his mouth against her neck. "This thing between us has always been there, and we were never over each other." He paused and then asked, "I'm in Abuja this week. I'm back on Friday. Can I see you on Friday?"

He kissed her forehead before releasing her, waiting for an answer to his question.

She nodded as she took a step back. "Friday is fine."

"It's a date," he remarked as he opened his car. "Don't back out, Zala," he warned as he slid into the driver's seat.

"I won't," she promised.

Chapter Eleven

Sure enough, her mother was waiting for her in the living room.

"Where is Zuri?" she asked.

"I sent her up with Nana to get ready for bed. I wondered when you would come in after seeing your guest off, but you were out there kissing him, making out for anybody to see."

Zala's temper flared immediately.

The words her mother had just thrown at her cut deeper than she expected.

Zala had the grace to look shamefaced.

"I'm sorry, Mum," she said, trying to calm her mother, who looked visibly upset.

"What are you sorry about? Sorry for acting like a horny teenager in public, with no care that your daughter might see you."

"That wasn't meant to happen; it just happened," Zala said quickly, her voice a mix of frustration and defensiveness. But her mother wasn't having it. She gave her a point- ed look, arms crossed, clearly unimpressed.

"No," her mother replied firmly, her tone cutting through the air. "It did not just happen. You need to take responsibility for your choices. How long have you been in Lagos? Your marriage ended a couple of months ago, and now you are already running around with Tseye, putting it out there like some desperate woman."

Zala saw red at her mother's comment, her anger flaring up uncontrollably. Without thinking, she snapped, her words coming out sharp and filled with fury.

"That man, Tseye, was the man I would have married! He was the love of my life until you and Dad decided I had to marry that brute! Yes, Dad came through when he heard Negasi hit me a few times and forced him to agree to a divorce! What do you know? Do you know I was beaten at least three times a week by him? Have you seen the scars on my body? Of course not!" She pointed at the scar on her eye. "I got this when he hit me with his watch, and that's after we found out that Zuri was not his child! Yes, Zuri is not his child!"

She turned to look at her mother, who's eyes were wide in shock.

"Are you surprised? I didn't even know that Zuri was not his child until she fell ill and needed blood! That's when it clicked that she was Tseye's! One week, I was happy with Tseye, and you knew that! You let me date him for years! Then, the next week, I was forced to marry Negasi! So dear mummy, if I act like a horny teenager, I am allowed, especially if I act horny with the man, I have never stopped loving! I would have married Tseye if family had not come between us!"

She was crying by the time she'd finished her outburst. She needed to vent; this was not how she had envisioned telling her mother about Zuri and Tseye, but her mother's comments about her acting like a horny teenager had set her off.

She didn't look at her mother; if she did, she would have seen that her mother was crying softly at all she had heard.

Wiping her tears, she said softly, still not looking at her mother.

She whispered, "I'm sorry for shouting, Mum, but I'm not sorry for what I felt with Tseye. I'll never apologise for that. I'm going to bed now, if it's okay."

Without looking at her mother and without waiting for a response, Zuri stepped out into the hallway, leaving the tension behind her like a heavy fog. When she entered her room, Zuri was already fast asleep, which wasn't surprising; her daughter loved her sleep.

For the first time since her divorce, she stripped her clothes and stood before the full-length mirror in her dressing room, her eyes filling with tears as she studied the scars that marred her once-perfect body.

And as she always did, she blamed herself for Negasi's behavior.

She hadn't been an excellent wife to him; she had been cold and unable to love him, which had brought out the worst in him. Although she knew that was not the case, she couldn't help asking herself;

What if?

What if she had loved him?

Sinking to the floor, Zala rocked herself as she cried.

* * *

Zuri was nowhere to be found when she woke.

Frowning, she sat up in bed, reaching for the bedside clock, closing her eyes when she saw it was almost 11 am.

She swung her legs out of bed, muttering under her breath just as the door opened and her mother walked in.

"Good morning, Mum," she muttered. "So sorry, I woke up late."

"It's Saturday; I decided to let you sleep in; you needed it after your outburst last night," Mariam Kebede explained as she took the seat next to the bed. "Why didn't you tell me, Zala?" her mother asked.

"Mum…"

"No, Zala, I let you speak last night; now it's your turn to listen. I'm your mother, for God's sake! You think I would have let that marriage happen if I knew how you really felt about Tseye?" Her mother's voice broke. "Why didn't you tell me anything about what was going on in your marriage, Zala?"

Her eyes filling with tears, Zala looked at her mum.

"I wanted to, but I thought you would blame me. I blamed myself, Mum; I felt it was my fault that if I had shown Negasi a little bit of love, maybe, just maybe, he wouldn't have been so cruel."

"How can you think that?" her mother whispered brokenly as she reached across to wipe her daughter's tears with her hand. "No man deserves to hit a woman; you told your dad that he had hit you twice or so; you never told us he hit you constantly."

"Dad would have killed him, Mum; look how Dad reacted when he heard Negasi hit me once; even his parents were disappointed."

"Oh Zala, we failed you." Her mother was crying now. "I failed you."

"Mum," Zala said, leaning forward to hold her mother's

hand. "Mum, you did not. I chose not to speak out, and when I finally did, you came through for me."

"We should have seen the signs; you became withdrawn, a shadow of your former self; we all thought it was the pressure of being in the limelight."

"But I made it out with Zuri, and you and Dad have been marvelous, getting me a job and a house here in Lagos; it's a new phase."

"You said he found out about Zuri when she needed blood? That was during her surgery, right?"

Zala nodded. "I was shocked when I learned that Zuri was not Negasi's child; Negasi lost it. It was bad enough that he knew about Tseye, and then finding out that Zuri was Tseye's child was the final straw. I couldn't lie; I told him that if Zuri wasn't his, Tseye was her dad." She touched the scar above her eye. "He hit me with his watch in anger."

"You told us you hurt yourself."

"I had to; Dad was so angry; I was afraid he would hurt Negasi."

She shuddered at the memory.

He had turned on her the moment they got home from the hospital, hitting her in the eye with his watch.

For the first time, she had fought back.

She had pushed him so hard he fell back against the sofa.

Then she had told him in a chilling tone that she would kill him the next time he laid a finger on her.

The following day, she called her father from the hospital and told him she wanted a divorce and that Negasi had hit her. She had never returned to the house she had shared with Negasi. After that phone call, her father whisked her and Zuri to the family house from the hospital.

Then he had gone after Negasi and beaten him to a pulp.

"Does Tseye know?"

Zala nodded. "He was angry at first that I kept it from him; I had no way of knowing; I was already pregnant when I married Negasi."

"I am confused; if Negasi knows Zuri is not his, why is he asking for shared custody?"

"He's just being petty, Mum. I will never allow him access to Zuri, and when I'm ready to deal with his request, he will hear from me."

"And you? Zala, how do you feel about all this?" her mother asked.

"Are you asking about Tseye Mum?" her daughter teased as her mother nodded and smiled.

"Yes, I am; I saw you with him yesterday, Zala."

Zala shrugged.

"I never stopped loving Tseye Mum; that's foolish, right? I just buried my feelings for him, and when I saw him again, the feelings I had just resurfaced. Do I know how he feels? No, I don't; I know he is still attracted to me though; Tseye is a topic for another day."

"Oh, Zala, you've been through so much, and it hurts that I am only finding out now. What you said about the scars broke me; you never said anything about them."

"They are a reminder that marriage is not for me," Zala replied, smiling sadly.

"Don't say that Zala."

"But it's true, Mum, I don't know who would want a scarred woman for a life partner."

"Zala, you are not scarred, and if you feel that way about relationships, is it wise to start something with Tseye? What if he wants more?"

"You know Lola asked me the same question?"

"And what did you tell her?"

"I told her nothing, but when I get to that bridge with Tseye, I will cross it." She paused, then said quietly, "Tseye has asked me about my scars; on Friday, when we meet up, I will tell him how I got them. Maybe, that's the first step to healing, and I don't want any secrets between us."

* * *

It was almost 6 p.m. on Friday evening when Zala finished her shift. The office was already quiet, nearly everyone having left for the day. As she stepped out of her workplace, she sighed, the cool evening air brushing against her skin.

Squinting, she turned towards the car park to see if her driver had arrived, that was when she saw him.

Tseye, waiting in the car park.

His eyes lit up the moment they met hers, and the sight of him made her heart flutter.

A smile instinctively spread across her face as he walked towards her.

"How was Abuja?" she asked.

"Boring," he grinned, leading her to his shiny black Ranger Rover Sport ride.

She laughed. "Work or pleasure?"

"Work, how can it be pleasure when you weren't there?" Tseye joked.

"Stop teasing." Zala said laughing.

"Hey, you asked!" He grinned at her as he drove onto the busy road, which was filling up with cars. He noticed that traffic was already building up as he maneuvered between two black SUVs and hissed under his breath.

Lagos traffic was a nightmare especially on Friday evenings. On most Fridays, he, Naade, and Eyimofe hung out in the office until the traffic died down before they headed home, but today, he had to leave early because he wanted to be with Zala.

"Where are we off to?" Zala asked.

He glanced at her briefly. "My house," he replied.

"Oh," was all she said.

"Scared of being alone in my flat with me?" he teased.

"Of course not." She answered immediately.

"Don't worry, I will be on my best behavior," he promised, flashing her a grin.

And he was.

He made her a very simple dinner.

After dinner, he led her to the living room, where he had placed cushions on the floor for them to sit. She sat down, crossing her legs, and he sat opposite her.

"So, what happened after I left that night? Did your mum grill you?"

"Oh, she did more than that; she called me a horny teenager," Zala chuckled. "She was shocked that I was making out in public."

Tseye threw back his head and laughed. "So, what did you say?"

"Oh, Tseye, I was angry. I said things to her that hurt her, but I was just angry, you know, looking for someone to blame."

"Why?" Tseye asked.

* * *

It was how he said it and how he looked at her when he asked why that made her open up to him.

"My marriage was horrible, Tseye."

She waited for him to say something, and when he didn't, she continued.

"He hit me constantly; any small thing set him off, and it only got worse when he found out about you. He went through my phone and found messages I had sent to Lola, telling her I missed you and that I'd made a mistake."

She looked away, pain filling her eyes as she recalled the horror of her marriage.

"I lived in constant fear. I couldn't tell my parents, but I told Lola, and she was livid, but what could she do when I refused to stand up for myself," she shook her head as she looked down at her hands; "I know you accused me of going from your bed to his when I told you about Zuri, you need to know that was not how it happened. The week after we broke up, I got engaged to Negasi. I can't say he forced himself on me, but I can tell you, I hated every moment of it; I told myself it was my duty as his fiancé, so I just lay there silent while he did it."

"Zala?" Tseye finally spoke; she looked up at him. "The scars? Tell me about them."

She nodded. "He hit me a lot" She smiled, her eyes shining with tears. "Looking back now, I realised I should have stood up for myself; if I had done so, maybe I wouldn't have so many scars."

Tseye moved and then kneeled before her as he reached for the buttons on her shirt.

"What are you doing?" she asked.

"Ssh." He placed a finger across her lips, pushing her hand away. Then he began unbuttoning her shirt, sliding it off so she was left wearing only her bra.

Then he bent down and touched the scar on her stomach with his finger before he bent down to kiss it.

"This scar does not make you ugly." He kissed her scar, then turned her around so he could see her back; he touched the scars on her back, kissing them lightly. "Neither does this make you undesirable."

"Tseye," she began, but he squeezed her shoulders to silence her.

"Your scars do not define you, and you are not scarred. They prove you are a strong and beautiful woman." He lifted her hair and kissed the back of her neck before reaching for her shirt to drape it over her before he began doing her buttons up.

"You think your scars are going to put me off? They only make me love you more because it proves you survived; any man who hits a woman is a coward; never forget that. A man can get his point across without raising his fist to hit a woman, and only cowards hit women."

He finished doing up her shirt and then hugged her, burying his face in her hair as she slid her arms around him. "I'm crazy about you. Zala, it will be hard to prove that to you, especially since we just reconnected, but I am ready to wait for you. This time, I am not letting you go."

He lifted his head and looked down at her. "Come to Dubai with me next week," he said. "Dubai?"

"Yes, Dubai, I have a meeting there three days. You could shop while I meet the team we are trying to recruit to run the new lounge the guys and I are opening. Then, when we come back, if you want, Zuri can meet my folks; what do you say?"

Zala remained silent for a moment, her thoughts swirling.

"I don't know, Tseye, this is all sudden," she said, shaking her head slightly. "It's a lot to think about. And Zuri, she's my priority, you know that."

He nodded, understanding. "Of course. I wouldn't ask you to do anything you're not comfortable with. But I want you to know that this... this isn't just about us. It's about creating a future, something we build together slowly. I want to be a part of your life, Zala. I let you go before; I am not willing to let that happen again."

She met his gaze, seeing the sincerity in his eyes. Part of her was still scared.

Part of her still held on to the pain from the past.

Another part of her wanted to let go and give in to Tseye.

"Tseye..." she began, stopping when he placed a finger against her lips.

"Shh," he said, bending over to kiss her. You don't have to say anything now. Just think about it and let me know, okay? I would love for you to come to Dubai with me."

Zala was tempted to say yes, but she couldn't.

She had Zuri to think about, and she had to ask her mum if it was okay to travel and leave Zuri with her.

"Hey, I am ready to wait for your answer," he teased as he sat back on his cushion, pulling her to settle against him, his arms going around to hold her in place.

"Dubai sounds like fun."

"It will be if you come along," he joked.

"I am supposed to be in Addis Ababa this week."

"Why?"

"Negasi is asking a judge to award him shared custody of Zuri, and it's looking like the judge might grant him that." She winced as she felt Tseye's arms tighten around her, indicating his displeasure.

However, when he spoke, his tone was calm. "Are you going to allow that?"

"No way, I kept quiet about Zuri, knowing it is a scandal his family wouldn't want, but I will tell him that if he insists, I will make it known that Zuri is not his daughter. Negasi wouldn't want that."

"Are you going to Addis Ababa?" he asked, and from his tone, she could tell he was worried for her.

"No way!" She shook her head and almost smiled when she heard his sigh of relief. "I'm not that dumb."

"I'm glad," he whispered, kissing the top of her head as she snuggled closer.

They spent the remainder of the evening talking, and when she told him it was time to leave, he drove her home and walked her to the door.

He kissed her and reminded her to let him know about the Dubai trip so he could buy their tickets.

Chapter Twelve

"She said yes to the Dubai trip," Tseye yelled as he hung up the call with Zala.

"Let me understand what you are saying; you have met Zuri, you and Zala are in a relationship, you are going to Dubai with her for three days, yet you haven't told your parents they have a granddaughter," Eyimofe said.

"Told his parents? Forget his parents; he hasn't even let us meet Zuri yet," Naade chirped in

"I am still in shock at how fast your life is moving and without brakes," Eyimofe muttered, shaking his head.

"Eyimofe is correct; at least apply brakes, and please tell your folks before you leave for Dubai, or have you forgotten Eyimofe's mum is in Dubai? Just imagine the phone call she would make if she ran into you and Zala."

Tseye pointed out, "Aunty is back tomorrow, so there's no

chance of me running into her."

"By the way, was that why you jumped at attending the meeting in Dubai when Naade was scheduled to attend it? So, you could go with Zala?" You are aware this is a business meeting, right?" Eyimofe asked.

"He's going to combine business with pleasure, of course. Did you not see the fist he made when Zala called him a couple of minutes ago?" Naade laughed at Eyimofe's expression.

"Guys, I'm sitting here. Can you stop talking about me like I'm not here?"

"Huh? There is no need to get excited; I am saying that you should do things in order: meet Zuri, introduce her to your parents and us, and then start dating Zala before the trip to Dubai." Eyimofe explained as though he were speaking to a kid.

"You are one to talk! Who was the one who went to Makurdi with my sister and immediately started dating her? Remind me again how my Mum and Aunty Nebi found out about you and Yahimba?"

"It's not the same thing, and there was no child involved, you oaf," grumbled Eyimofe.

"Ah, it's the same thing; both of you are sneaky when it comes to relationships, dating in secret until something happens" Naade smirked, looking from Eyimofe to Tseye.

"Whose side are you on, Naade?" Eyimofe snapped.

"The side of truth" was Naade's reply as Tseye burst out laughing at the look on Eyimofe's face.

"I am on the side of truth, look, if you want to go to Dubai, Tseye, by all means, do so, but you need to tell your folks about Zuri before they find out from another source. That would not be fair to your parents." Naade repeated.

"I know, guys; I just don't know how to start that conversation," Tseye responded.

"You are not at fault here; you never knew about Zuri. Your parents also knew how broken up you were when Zala left to get married; hmm, that's another issue, Zala again, back in your life? That will be a hard sell, especially to your Mum.," said Eyimofe

Tseye nodded at Eyimofe. "Now you understand why I am in a fix. I am just going to take Zala to Dubai, and when I get back, I will deal with my folks."

"That," Naade said, pointing at Tseye, "is a wise decision"

"You think?" Tseye muttered, looking at his friends.

Eyimofe nodded. "Knowing your mum and my mum, Naade is correct; that's the best decision for now."

"Pfft. I never knew I had such cowards as friends. I thought you said there was an order to do things.

What happened to the order of doing things?" Tseye said to Eyimofe, who shrugged.

"That was before we remembered that your mum would probably hate that Zala is back in your life after her divorce." Eyimofe was quick to reply.

"Bloody cowards," Tseye swore at his friends.

"We accept that tag, don't we, Eyimofe?" Naade turned to ask Eyimofe.

"The coward tag? Oh yes, we do, with honors, too," Eyimofe joked.

* * *

Dubai had always been and would always be one of her favorite cities.

She first visited Dubai with Tseye, Naade, and Eyimofe and remembered it as one of the best holidays ever. It had been Eyimofe's birthday, and they had decided to celebrate in Dubai. Of course, she and Tseye had been a couple, and Eyimofe had been with Tayo then. Speaking of Tayo, she wondered where she was.

Was she still with Eyimofe?

"Remember the last time we were here for Eyimofe's birthday party?" she asked as they waited outside the Dubai International Airport for the chauffeur.

"Yes, that was an amazing party." Tseye smiled at the

memory.

"Yes, it was. What about Tayo? Are she and Eyimofe still together?"

"Tayo?" Tseye looked amused. "He and Tayo broke up; Eyimofe is with Yahimba."

"Yahimba? As in, Yahimba your sister?"

"Yes." He nodded as they got into the car.

"Eyimofe is dating your sister?" she asked again. Tseye gave an amused look.

"You look surprised."

She shook her head as the vehicle slowly pulled from the curb and left the airport.

"Where are we staying?" she asked quietly, changing the topic.

"Jumeirah Beach Hotel," he replied. I got a suite." Turning to face her, he asked, "Is that okay?"

"That's fine," she answered before looking out the window, her heart beating fast as they sped toward the hotel.

When they were shown to their suites, Tseye apologized and said he had to meet with their partners at the pool bar to review their plans for the next meeting.

He leaned over and kissed her forehead.

"You are here to have fun, relax, and go shopping. Once I'm done with my meeting, we can have dinner at the hotel's Italian restaurant. I hear the food is excellent. Before you say anything or argue, I left my credit card by your handbag; please use it if you have to." He winked at her before turning and leaving the suite.

Left to her own devices, she first called her mother to let her know she had arrived safely. Then, she spoke to an excited Zuri, who was eager to hear about her trip.

After getting off the phone with her Mum, she took a shower and settled down to call Lola, who had left her a voicemail asking how her trip was.

"About time," Lola snapped when she finally got through to her. "How was your trip?"

"It was good."

"And Tseye?" Lola asked. Zala chuckled.

"What about Tseye?"

"You know what I am asking about."

"It's a business trip, Lola," Zala explained, laughing.

"Yeah, right, so I suppose you are staying in different rooms then?"

"Nope, we got a suite."

"A suite!" Lola squealed. "Hmm, Zala."

Zala shook her head as Lola chuckled on the other end of the phone.

"You have a dirty mind, Lola! I just called to let you know I got in okay and will call you later. I'm going to get something to eat."

"Haha, have fun, and call me when you can." Her friend laughed as she hung up.

Shaking her head, Zala dressed up to go to the Dubai Mall.

She loved shopping, and the Dubai Mall was one of her favorite places to shop; she glanced at Tseye's card next to her handbag and smiled; she wouldn't use it. Slipping on a pair of white sandals to match her red and white shift dress, she picked up her bag and left the suite.

It was hot as usual, hot and sweltering, and she was only too glad to get into the cab that the reception had waiting for her.

Glad she was headed to the mall; she smiled in anticipation as she thought of all the shops in the air-conditioned shopping mall. Soon, she got to the mall sighing with relief as she exited her cab. As she entered the shopping mall, the cool air swept across her face, leaving her with a refreshing sensation.

"Ah, bliss," she murmured as she gazed around the bustling beehive of activities.

One of the largest malls in the UAE and the world, the Dubai Mall was a shopper's delight.

You could never be bored in the Dubai Mall.

She thought to herself as she began calculating which shop to visit first. Two hours later, she smiled to herself as she strolled through the bustling mall, her steps light and relaxed. The sound of footsteps and soft chatter surrounded her as she made her way to the concierge section, where she would inquire about getting a cab back to her hotel. The warmth of the day lingered on her skin, and for a brief moment, everything felt perfect

She had bought a purse for her Mum and Lola, a handbag for herself and a couple of dresses for Zuri. She felt guilty at the amount of money she was spending out of her savings, but she hadn't bought anything for herself in the last two years, and she deserved a treat.

Tseye was back in the suite when she got back to the hotel.

He glanced at her and grinned when he saw the amount of bags she was carrying.

"Someone's been busy," he said, helping with some of the bags she was carrying.

"It was worth it." She grinned up at him. "Have you eaten yet?"

"I was waiting for you," he answered as she suddenly yawned. "We can eat in the restaurant tomorrow if you want; you look tired."

"Please, can we dine in? I'm too tired to go down," she pleaded.

Tseye nodded. "I'll let you settle down, and then I'll order our dinner to be sent to the suite."

"Thank you. How was your meeting?" she asked as she headed towards the room.

"Today's meeting went well. Tomorrow, we start at 9 a.m. and finish at 1 p.m., and then I'm all yours for the rest of the day."

By the time she emerged from the shower, Tseye had organized dinner.

Grateful because she was tired and hungry, she sat down to eat. Dinner was fun; Tseye told her about his and his friends' plans for the lounge, which they hoped would be open by December in time for Christmas in Lagos.

Christmas in Lagos was fun.

She'd experienced it twice and was amazed at the energy Nigerians put into partying during that period.

Then, in January, it was back to the grind.

She could sense his excitement as he explained their plans for the lounge, and she was happy for them. Contrary to what people thought, Tseye and his friends had worked hard to achieve success in their business.

She was looking forward to the opening of their Lounge. By the time dinner was over, she was yawning, and he smiled as he said quietly;

"You go off; I will sort this mess out."

She smiled apologetically. "Are you sure?"

He nodded, "Yes I am; besides I have some documents to go through."

"Thank you, Tseye."

Chapter Thirteen

His meeting the following day took longer than expected.

He felt terrible because she was still fast asleep when he left just before Nine.

At 4 p.m., he texted her again, apologizing that his meetings had taken longer than expected and promising to be back in time for them to have dinner at Nuska Beach. She texted back, saying she had spent the day at the pool and would be ready for dinner when he got back.

He smiled, texting back that he had booked their table for 6 pm.

She sent him a cheeky emoji.

She was ready when he walked in, and he immediately got changed.

"I was hoping to spend the day with you; I had no idea that the meeting would take so long," he apologized when they were seated at their table.

"How did it go?" she asked.

He shook his head. "Not going as, we expected, but fingers crossed, we should wrap things up tomorrow."

She reached across to tap his hand, and he felt a jolt of electricity.

"It will," she said.

She had kept him awake most of the night, with her tossing and clinging to him, driving him nuts; he had woken up with a nagging headache from lack of sleep.

Forcing himself to smile and control his wayward emotions, he said, "We should order."

It was either that, or he would pull her up and march her back to their suite, where he'd indulge in every desire that had been building up inside him, and give in to every unspoken craving he'd been struggling to control.

* * *

"We should order." It was as though he had been eager to eat and return to the suite.

Dinner had been nice, but Tseye had been reserved, speaking only when spoken to. Yes, he had been his usual charming self, but he was reserved.

It was as if he was holding himself back from her.

"I'm going to take a shower," he said immediately after they got into their suite. She watched him quickly disappear into the shower, closing the door behind him.

She was talking to her mum on the phone when he emerged. He nodded towards her, indicating he was done, smiling as she pointed at her phone and disappeared into the shower.

She would not let him ignore her; she decided as she hung up her call and started showering; after toweling herself dry, she slid on the housecoat provided, tying the belt, she left the shower room.

When she emerged from the shower, he was standing by the bed, dressed in grey pajama bottoms. Without saying a word, she marched up to him, pulling his head down to hers, and kissed him.

* * *

Tseye had been struggling to keep his arms to himself all day, trying to be the perfect gentleman so as not to scare her and push her away until he was sure she was ready.

So, he was caught off guard when she walked up to him and kissed him. His surprise lasted for a split second, and then his arms slid around her as he kissed her back.

Oh, God, help me, he thought as her hands slid over his shoulders, touching him as she demanded he kiss her back. Something unfurled within him as soon as she touched his collarbone, and his mouth opened over hers as she kissed him back. Her mouth on his was heaven-sent, and he couldn't get enough of her.

All he could think of was how she could make him feel things he hadn't felt in a long time. He held her hand against him, and she moaned against him as he pressed her hard against him.

"Zala," he said in between kisses, "Do you want me to stop?" he groaned.

"Never," she whispered. "Don't stop, please."

That was all he needed to hear.

He reached down and undid the belt of her toweling robe and slid it off her; his breath caught in his throat as she stood naked before him.

She moved, kissing him again, and he kissed her back as his hands roamed over her perfect body. Her scent overtook his nostrils, filling him with promise and anticipation as he remembered how they had been in the past. Breaking the kiss, he swung her off her feet, carrying her across the room; he placed her on the bed as he took off his pants.

Then, lying next to her, he rolled her on top of him, pulling her head down so he could kiss her as he wanted to. His tongue dueled with hers, demanding a submission she offered willingly as he cupped her breasts, delighting in her moans. When she reached down to touch his stomach again, he moved, rolling her beneath him as he lifted her to him.

Then he did what he had been dreaming of: he took her again and again, hammering into her so hard and fast that he thought she would break, but she matched him, thrust for thrust, kissing him hard as they moved in unison. God help me, he thought as he held her waist, hammering into her, his head buried in the nape of her neck, delighting in her moans; he kissed her until he felt her hurtling over.

His mouth closed over hers, capturing her scream as she came; then he shuddered as he followed soon after, emptying himself into her.

He hadn't used a condom, she realised.

He hadn't used one the last time, either.

"What are you thinking about?" he asked, kissing her.

"We didn't use protection," she replied, her eyes wide.

"I'm safe, Zala," Tseye said, touching her cheek with the tip of his finger.

"Oh" was all she said as he grinned cheekily.

"What are you scared of?" he said as his hands moved down her body to touch her scars.

Her breath caught in her throat as his head followed his hands. He kissed her scars, his fingers tracing them.

She shuddered as he began kissing his way back up; the heat was starting to spread through her body again as he kissed her slowly everywhere, covering her body with his; he looked up as their eyes met.

She didn't need to say anything except give herself up to the pleasure he was wrecking within her, with his hands and mouth. By the time she he slid into her again, she was ready and waiting.

* * *

Tseye woke her up with a kiss. "You haven't left yet?" She yawned.

"No, the meeting was rescheduled to 1 pm."

"That's good then," she muttered, swinging her feet off the bed as she got out; still clutching the sheet, he turned to face him.

"What do you want to do?" she asked him.

He glanced down at his watch. "I have three hours till my next meeting; we could do breakfast."

"Twenty minutes," she said, smiling as she dropped the sheet and hurried into the shower.

She winced and went hot all over as she saw the bite marks on her neck and the slope of her breast. Last night had been fantastic. She hadn't felt like this in years.

Married life with Negasi had been horrible, and in the last

couple of months, she had avoided him and never given him the opportunity for them to be intimate.

Her mouth thinned in disgust as she thought of Negasi. She would have to deal with him sooner or later, but for now, she would ignore him and his legal team and get on with her life. Her life, which now included Tseye.

Tseye was waiting for her when she emerged from the shower, fully dressed twenty minutes later.

"I'm ready."

He nodded, holding out his hand, which she took and followed him out of their suite.

They had breakfast in one of the many restaurants in the Jumeirah Beach Hotel, and then Tseye wanted to visit the mall to get a gift for his parents for their wedding an-anniversary.

"Are your folks having a party for it?"

"You bet, my dad and I insisted." He looked down at her. "Heads up, you and Zuri will attend."

"Do you think that's wise?" she asked as she bit her lower lip. "You haven't told them about Zuri."

"I haven't told my parents about you and Zuri," he corrected. "There's no way I can introduce Zuri to my parents without mentioning you, and after last night, there's no negotiation, you will meet my parents as the woman I am dating."

"You've forgotten I have already met your parents," she pointed out.

"Zala, stop worrying, your pretty head and relax, my parents don't bite, okay? They have always liked you."

"That was before I dumped you and married Negasi," she grumbled.

He threw back his head and laughed.

"Oh, so you finally agreed that you dumped me?" he teased.

"Didn't you tell everybody who cared to listen that I dumped you? When the truth was that we broke up."

"I don't recall breaking up with you; if I remember correctly, you marched into my apartment, broke up with me and left without a care in the world."

"Hmm," she hissed, elbowing him in the ribs. "Any way you spin it, your parents will see me as the woman who dumped their son and married someone else, and now she is divorced and back with his child. It's not a very nice story, Tseye."

Tseye sighed.

"I know that Zala, but we will handle this when we return to Lagos. I will speak to my parents. My mum may take a while to accept you. I'm not going to lie to you about how she will react, but I know that as long as we want this, she will come around. So, give us a chance, okay?"

"Tseye?"

"Trust me on this, Zala. Please."

Tseye stopped and turned to face her. He slid his hands into his pockets and rocked back on his heels.

"I believe you, Tseye; I'm just scared."

"Don't be; just trust me," Tseye flashed her a grin. "It's all going to work out fine; now let's go and have fun; we just have this night before we get back to the real world and face my folks."

* * *

His parents were in the living room when he got to their family house, and they were surprised to see him so late, especially as he had just returned from Dubai.

"Did you come straight from the airport?" Chief Omadoye asked as Tseye bent down to kiss his Mum on her cheek.

"Not really. I had to drop a friend off, and I needed to talk to you both."

"What is so important that you couldn't wait till tomorrow? You just got back from Dubai, and you must be tired.," Alero Harriman said as Tseye took the seat opposite them, stretching out his legs.

"Alero, let the young man be. He said he wanted to see us," his father scolded his wife, shaking his head when she gave him a warning look.

"Tseye?" she asked, turning back to face her son.

Tseye held back a smile; he had expected her questions; his mum had the uncanny ability to sense if something was wrong; well, he hoped she would not blow a gasket when she heard what he had to say.

"I went to Dubai," he said.

"Yes, we know. So?" his mother said.

He took a deep breath and said, "It was a business meeting, but I went with a lady friend, and we spent the last three days together." He paused and said, "It's serious; I'm serious about her."

As expected, his dad said nothing, but not his Mum; he knew she had a lot of questions, and the look of surprise on her face had him smiling inwardly.

"Serious? Since when? When did you start dating her, and why haven't we met her? I didn't know you were in a relationship" She glanced at her husband, "Did you know about this Doye?"

"I am as surprised as you; which of the questions do you want him to answer first?" her husband responded to her question with his question.

Alero Harriman turned back to her son, who was watching his parents bicker, and demanded, "If you are so serious about her, why haven't we met her yet?"

"You've met her," Tseye responded.

"We have?" his father said, sitting up as his wife turned to look at him and then back at Tseye.

"We have?" she repeated her husband's question.

Tseye took a deep breath, willing himself to be calm. "You've met her; it's Zala Kebede."

The silence that followed his comment was deafening, and you could hear a pin drop.

Looking up, his eyes clashed with his mother's, and for the first time, he wished he had his friends here to support him; this would be a long night.

He heard her gasp before she spoke, "What is the name of the lady who accompanied you to Dubai?"

"Alero…" his father began, but his mother held up her hand and cut him off mid-sentence.

"Doye, please. I asked you a question, Tseye."

"Mum, you heard me, I went to Dubai with Zala Kebede."

"Zala Kebede? Isn't she married?" was his mother's reply to his comment.

"She's divorced," Tseye explained, glancing at his father for moral support, but Chief Omadoye shook his head.

"She's divorced? So, she left you for another man, gets divorced, and then she comes back to you, and you both continue from where you left off, is that it?" his mother snapped.

"That is not what happened, Mum."

"Really?" she asked, looking away from her son and toward her husband. "Are you going to say something about this?"

Chief Omadoye shrugged. He knew better than to get involved when his wife was angry.

"Alero, let's hear him out first," Chief Omadoye said quietly.

"Hear him out; he just told us he is dating his ex, who left him for another man; what could be worse than that?"

"Mum," he said, groaning as she shot him furious look; "That's not all, Mum."

"What else is there to say? Are you going to tell me she is pregnant with your child?"

At her question, Tseye almost groaned out aloud.

"No, she's not pregnant, but she does have a four-year- old daughter, Zuri. And I recently discovered that Zuri is my daughter."

Tseye glanced at his father, whose mouth had dropped open in shock, and then he glanced at his mother, who looked at him like he were the devil himself.

Then Chief Omadoye stood from his seat. "I think a drink is needed"

"Please, sit down, Doye," Alero Harriman said, her tone firm yet controlled. "Could you repeat what you just said, Tseye?"

"I have a daughter, Zuri, and she's almost four; I only just found out."

"I heard that. I need you to confirm who your child's mother is.," his mother said.

"Mum, I have a child with Zala."

"Good. You have confirmed that, and are you dating Zala Kebede again?"

Tseye nodded.

"The same Zala who left you for another man?" Alero Harriman asked.

"She had a reason, Mum."

"She had a reason. Is that what she told you? Are you really this foolish, Tseye?"

Tseye got to his feet; "Mum, listen to me, please?"

"No, you listen to me! Why should I? So, this is how it is with the men in this family? Children outside wedlock? At least I'm meeting your daughter as a child, not as an adult!"

"Mum!"

"What? Am I wrong? It's beginning to look like a trend amongst the men in my family! Springing children on me!" his mother retorted.

"That's low, Alero," her husband said quietly from beside her, his voice steady but laced with disapproval.

"You know what?" she said. "I am going to bed. I am glad you had a good trip. It's late. You better go home." She looked at her husband. "Doye, not another word from you, not one word; good night, Tseye."

Chief Omadoye waited until she left the living room, then turned to his son and sighed. "It didn't occur to you to speak to me first before springing this on your mother? You know your mother, Tseye, you should have called me first to tell me."

"I thought it was best to tell you both at the same time."

"Next time, before you think it's wise to spring something like this on us, tell me first, okay?"

"Next time? Dad, are you expecting me to have another child from a different woman?"

"Shut up, Tseye."

"Just asking Dad," Tseye chuckled.

Chief Omadoye shook his head, a smile on his face.

"Dad, what will I do?" his son asked quietly.

Chief Omadoye got to his feet and walked over to pat his son on the shoulder.

"Leave it to me. I know how to handle your mother. Go home. I will speak to her and call you tomorrow. Tseye, I hope you know what you're doing. This Zala lady has already hurt you once. Do you think getting involved with her again is wise?"

"Dad, I know how this looks, and I know Zala messed up in the past. I will not defend her actions, but I know whatever happened then was not entirely her fault. This time, I admit I practically seduced her into a relationship with me. All I am saying is I have forgiven her. I have a daughter with her, and I would love for you and Mum to meet Zuri and give Zala a chance."

"I will speak to your Mum," his father promised. "Thanks, Dad."

Chapter Fourteen

The following weekend, Tseye spent the Saturday with Zuri and Zala.

He took Zuri to The Flower Shop, which was becoming her favorite restaurant because of their waffles.

They still hadn't told her he was her father.

He watched as Zala lifted their laughing daughter into the air, twirling her around with effortless grace. The sound of her laughter filled the air, and he couldn't help but smile. His heart swelled with warmth and a deep overwhelming sense of love as he watched them together, so full of joy, so perfectly at ease. It was a moment that felt timeless, a picture of happiness that stirred something deep within him.

This was where he wanted to be with Zuri and Zala.

He was amazed at how Zala changed when she was with Zuri. Her whole face lit up, and you could feel her love for her daughter in every word and gesture.

With him, she was different, nervous and jumpy.

She only let herself go when she was in bed with him, and he hated that.

He hated that the only time he saw a glimpse of the old Zala was in bed when she was in his arms.

Outside his bed, she was reserved, nervous, and jumpy around him; it was as though she was waiting for him to explode and get angry, and it killed him inside every time he saw the wary look in her eyes. It hurt that she thought he would hit her.

He had never laid a finger on her and never would.

He was desperate to help and get her to speak to him; since they had spoken about Negasi the first day, she had not discussed it again.

It hurt and annoyed him to think that any man would hit a woman to the point that she would lose confidence in herself as Zala had.

He had to do something to help her and get her to believe in herself.

Zala had always been carefree, outgoing and bubbly, and he would not allow anybody to kill her beautiful spirit.

He was ready to wait; he would, no matter how long it took her to heal.

Deep down, he knew that being intimate with him was her way of escaping from her thoughts, but for him, it was love.

He had fallen in love with Zala Kebede all over again and that love was what he would show her and help her heal.

* * *

After they had dropped Zuri home, he asked, "Do you want to come out for a drink? Or would you rather go to my place?"

"We could go to yours," she said.

He nodded, starting the car, and drove off towards Banana Island. As soon as he walked into his apartment, he locked the door and pulled her into his arms, burying his nose in her hair.

"I've missed you" he whispered.

"I was with you last week; we spent three days in Dubai. Have you already forgotten?"

"I haven't seen you since the day we got back, and that was four days ago."

"We talk every day, every night," she protested, laughing as she pulled back.

"Not enough," he said, bending his head and kissing her, coaxing her lips apart, sighing as she opened to him to allow him access. "I haven't kissed you since or held you like this," he muttered as he cupped her breasts, kissing her as she moaned.

"You drive me crazy, Zala; that hasn't changed."

* * *

Well, it hadn't changed for her either, she realised as he kissed her again and again, nibbling at her bottom lip.

She grabbed his shirt to stop her from falling as he moved her against the wall, pressing her against the wall as he stopped kissing her.

"I brought you here for a drink, and that's all we are going to do, have a drink," he said.

"No," she responded, kissing him under the chin.

"Yes, Zala, it's a drink, then home to Zuri and your mum. I'm still trying to get into your Mum's good books.," he laughed, straightening her shirt.

"Then you shouldn't have kissed me," she joked.

"Aren't you a naughty girl? A kiss doesn't always have to lead to that," he teased.

"With the way you kiss Tseye? God, help me!" she grumbled as he pulled her away from the wall.

Tseye laughed, pulling her close as she led her to the kitchen to get the drink he promised her.

"I have to get you back home early; remember, I am trying to get on your Mum's good side."

"Good luck with that."

Tseye grinned as he poured her a drink.

"You mentioned you spoke to your parents about Zuri; how did it go?"

"You want the truth?" Zala nodded. "Of course."

"My Mum is not speaking to me; she's not answering my calls."

"Oh. Are you okay?"

"No, I'm not. I am a bit upset because she's not answering my calls. I know my mother has a right to be upset with me because we are still dealing with the issue of my sister. Then I tell her I have a child."

"Tseye, how would you have wanted her to react? I was dating you, broke up, and married someone else. I am now divorced and back in your life with a child I claim to be yours. Tell me, what mother would want that for her son?" Zala asked.

"Really, what would you do if you were in her shoes."

Zala took a deep breath. "I would insist on a DNA test, Tseye."

"How would you have felt if I had asked you for one?"

169

"Tseye, I would have done it so you wouldn't have any concern, but I know Zuri is yours; I have only been intimate with two men in my life, you and my ex, and Zuri is not his; he already had a DNA test done," she responded honestly.

"You do know that eventually you will have to have one done to prove I am her father if you are going to have to face Negasi in court and say he is not her father," Tseye remarked.

Zala nodded, closing her eyes briefly as she thought of what Tseye had just said.

Why was life so complicated?

How had she allowed herself to be put in such a precarious situation?

Zala loved her dad and would do anything for him; unfortunately, this time, helping her dad had come at the expense of her happiness.

"Zala?"

She opened her eyes and looked at Tseye.

"What's going through that pretty head of yours?" he asked, stroking her cheek.

"I'm sorry, Tseye." "Hey, what for?"

"All this is happening because of me, I should have stayed away and gone to America like I originally intended."

"And keep me from meeting Zuri?" "What if you had been married, Tseye?"

"I'm not married. Listen, Zala, getting back together will not be easy for our parents to accept, but we will get through this. I expected my mum to react like this, babe; she is still getting over my dad having a daughter."

"Yes, your sister Yahimba, what's she like?"

"She's okay, I guess, but she doesn't want to know or get closer to us, which hurts, but hey, that's her choice and my folks and I respect that."

Zala sat up, surprised. "You mentioned she is dating Eyimofe?"

"She is," replied Tseye, wondering where she was going with her question.

"How is that going to work? How is she going to date Eyimofe and keep away from you? Eyimofe is practically family; his mum and your mum are best friends."

Tseye shrugged, pouring himself a drink. "She needs time to accept us."

Like his mum needed to come to terms with the fact that she had reappeared in his life and with a child.

She told herself she would never be good enough for Tseye as her insecurities resurfaced. Maybe in the past, but not now, with a divorce behind her, her scars, and a child in tow. Tseye's mother may have loved her in the past, but now she was dam- aged goods, and no mother would want that for her son.

* * *

"Ah! So, you still remember you have a job?" Naade exclaimed when Tseye walked into the office Monday morning.

"Good morning to you, too, and what the hell is that supposed to mean?" Tseye retorted. "I was here Thursday, and we hung out on Friday."

Eyimofe glanced at his watch. "It's Monday, and you stroll in at 11 am looking like you won the lottery. You are late, Tseye."

"I'm sorry, guys, I slept in, that's all."

Naade waited for him to sit and reach for a mug to pour himself a cup of tea. Then, casually, he remarked, "Aunty Alero is waiting in the small office we use for lunch."

"What?!" Tseye shot up, dropping the cup back with a clatter; wincing as the hot liquid splashed on his hand. "My Mum is here?"

"That's what he said," replied Eyimofe, nodding toward the office Naade had mentioned.

"Shit! Shit!" Tseye swore softly as he walked out of the office to see his mother.

His mum was reading a magazine when he walked into the small office they used for lunch.

"Good morning, Mum; I had no idea you were coming today," he said.

"Sit down, Tseye."

Tseye immediately sat; he had no intention of exchanging words with her; if his mum said jumped, he would jump. "I have been calling you since Friday. Did you choose to ignore me?" he asked.

"With good reason, and you didn't have the common sense to come to the house if you wanted to talk to me?" his mother asked, placing the magazine on the table beside her seat.

"That's true, I should have come by the house" her son mumbled, looking ashamed.

"So why didn't you?" Alero Harriman asked.

That was a good question. He almost smiled; his Mum knew him so well.

"You were avoiding me," she said quietly.

He couldn't help it, he smiled. "Yes, I was; your reaction scared me."

"How did you expect me to react? You brought Zala home four years ago and introduced her as the lady you wanted to marry; I accepted her as a daughter, and then she broke your heart. A week after she broke up with you, she was en- gaged to be married. This is a lady you dated for over three years. Now, she's divorced and back with a child, your child! Tseye, did you have a DNA test done to confirm her claims?"

"I didn't, Mum," he mumbled, not sure how she would react to his answer.

"How do you know she is yours?" he wasn't surprised at her question; he expected her to ask.

"She didn't even know Zuri was mine until some months back; Zuri was ill and needed blood; her husband wasn't a match, so he had a DNA done. That was one of the reasons she asked for a divorce."

"One of the reasons? What other reason could there be? Do you know why she got divorced?"

"Mum, that's Zala's story to tell."

"Tseye, you and your dad have put me through a lot. First, there is Yahimba, who wants nothing to do with us and is dating my best friend's son. Then you have decided to reconcile with your ex, who has so much baggage. You and your dad have been very busy."

"Mum, I'm happy with Zala; shouldn't that be all that matters?" her son said.

She sighed. "Tseye, I know you never got over Zala; you haven't dated or had any serious relationship since she broke up with you, which is why I am worried. I am concerned that you may just be holding onto memories and think it's love you feel. Are you sure about this?" his mother asked

"I am," her son responded.

"And Zala, she feels the same way?"

"She does; you haven't mentioned Zuri?"

"What about her?" his mother asked.

"Would you like to meet her?" he asked.

"If I say no, what will you do?" his mother responded. "I will keep asking," Tseye grumbled, glaring at his mother.

"Asking me if I want to meet your daughter is foolish. She is my granddaughter; why wouldn't I want to meet her? Your dad and I would like to meet Zuri if that's okay with Zala but don't expect me to jump for joy when Zala comes over. I will be courteous, but it will take a while for me to warm up to her" She paused and glared at her son. "Of all the women in Lagos, you decide to return to your ex, and Eyimofe decides he wants to be with Yahimba; what is wrong with you all?"

Tseye grinned. "The heart wants what it wants, Mum."

Chapter Fifteen

It's okay to be nervous, Zala told herself as she stood before the full-length mirror, thinking of Tseye's parents. " it's perfectly okay to be nervous."

She had opted to wear a peach dress with cap sleeves.

The bodice was fitted but gave way at the waist, its full skirt stopping just below her knees.

Contrary to what she told Tseye, she wasn't looking forward to meeting his parents again.

Far from it, she was nervous because she didn't know what to expect.

"Mummy, are you ready?" Zuri came running into her room, looking pretty in a light blue dress. Looking at her daughter, Zala could not understand how she had not seen the resemblance to Tseye until now.

Had she been so blind?

"Yes, I am. We just have to wait for Uncle Tseye to come and pick us up."

Zuri cocked her head to one side as she nibbled on her thumb.

"Where is he taking us to, Mummy?"

This was it, Zala decided as she sat on her bed and patted the space next to her.

"Come and sit here, Zuri."

"No, I will sit on your lap," her daughter grinned at her and climbed onto her lap.

Zala smiled as she moved her daughter from her lap to the bed and turned her around to face her.

"Zuri, remember I told you we would live in Nigeria now?"

Her daughter nodded, her ponytail dancing around her face.

"I like Nigeria; they have nice waffles," she told her mum.

"They do, Zuri. Do you remember I told you we would be living in Nigeria now?"

Zuri nodded again, her ponytails bouncing.

"Zuri, Uncle Tseye is taking us to see his parents." Zala took a deep breath, her fingers absently brushing her daughter's hair as she tried to find the right words. This conversation felt like a minefield she'd avoided for a while, but now it was time to face it head-on.

She couldn't delay the truth any longer.

"Zuri, baby, what if I told you Uncle Tseye is your daddy... your other daddy" she began, trying to be gentle but firm at the same time.

Zuri looked up at her, confused, and Zala could see the wheels turning in her head.

"Uncle Tseye is my Daddy? But I have a daddy." Zuri said to her mum.

"Zuri," Zala began softly, her voice gentle yet firm, as she knelt down to her daughter's level, "I know this is confusing, baby. You've always had another dad, but Uncle Tseye, whom you've been spending time with lately, is your real daddy."

Zuri's brow furrowed; her small voice filled with confusion. "But... but Daddy is at home. He's in Addis Ababa, in the big house."

Zala's heart twisted at the innocent misunderstanding, but she steadied herself. "No, Zuri," she said, her voice quiet but resolute. "Uncle Tseye is your daddy. Something happened, and he couldn't live with us, so we had to say in Addis Ababa."

Zuri's eyes searched her mother's face for answers, her

little hands clutching at the fabric of Zala's dress. "Why? If he's my daddy, why couldn't he live with us? What about Daddy, who's back at home?"

Her words pierced through Zala, leaving her momentarily speechless. Zuri's reference to Negasi as "Daddy" caught her off guard. Not only had Negasi been an absent and emotionally distant father, but Zuri had always been terrified of him, always avoiding him, always seeking comfort from Zala, not Negasi. Zala had never imagined that her daughter still viewed him in that light.

"I like Uncle Tseye; he is nice, but why is he, my Daddy?"

It was an innocent question, yet Zala had no idea how to explain.

Things were getting more complicated than she expected. Zuri tilted her head and looked at her mother as though she were trying to understand. "Mummy, I like Uncle Tseye. He's nice to me. He brings me waffles, and he plays with me."

Zala smiled, her heart aching with a mix of pride and sorrow.

"Yes, baby, Uncle Tseye is very kind to you, right?" She gently cupped Zuri's face as she kissed her forehead. "And he wants to be your daddy now, Zuri. He's going to be there for you from now on. You won't be alone, I promise."

Zuri looked at her mother, still processing everything, and

then she asked, "Will he stay with us?"

Zala nodded, her voice a little shakier than she wanted it to be.

"Yes, baby. He's here to stay. We'll be together, and you'll get to know him better."

The little girl seemed to accept this for the moment.

She cuddled closer to Zala, resting her head against her mother's chest.

"Mummy?" Zuri said, "Are you saying I have another daddy? And more grandparents, too?"

Zala nodded. "Yes, Zuri, you do, and we will meet them today."

"Yippee!" Zuri squealed, a smile breaking out on her face. "Will they buy me toys, sweets and ice cream? Grandma Abebe always buys me toys whenever I go to her house, and she makes me nice waffles too," she chirped, excited, forget- ting her confusion at being informed she had another father. Not surprised at how children's minds worked, Zala shook her head. Zuri adored Negasi's mother and had loved spending weekends in their house.

What's it with kids and grandparents these days?

"I am so excited, Mummy," her daughter squealed as she skipped beside her mother.

* * *

In the end, there was nothing to worry about.

Alero Harriman was welcoming and didn't hide her delight at meeting Zuri, who was enthralled by the size of her grandparents' house.

She was even more excited when she saw they had a pool.

Zala smiled as she remembered how Zuri had acted when Tseye had shown up.

"Mummy said you are my Daddy?" she asked, thumb in mouth as she looked up at Tseye.

Tseye nodded, ruffling her hair. "Yes, I am." He bent to her level as she squinted at him. "Nice to meet you, Zuri; I am your dad," he said, touching her cheek.

Zuri smiled brightly as she flung her tiny arms around his neck. "I already like you, Uncle Tseye." She hugged him.

"I like you too," Tseye whispered, his eyes filled with tears.

Sitting across from Tseye's parents, she felt her heart twist with pain as Chief Omadoye and Alero Harriman chatted with her daughter, delighting in her stories.

This could have been her life, and they could have been her family.

"Are you okay?" Tseye asked, sitting beside her. Zala nodded. "I am fine."

"You haven't said much since we got here," he pointed out

quietly.

Zala looked down at her fingers, her hair falling to the side, hiding her face from his view.

"There is nothing to say, Tseye." "Zala?"

She looked up, and their eyes met.

"I am glad your parents have accepted Zuri. It means a lot to her and to me, too."

Tseye reached across and took her hands in his, "They've accepted you too, Zala."

She shook her head, smiling sadly.

"Your mother was polite, very reserved towards me. She used to be so excited to see me; you and I know that's not the case now."

"Zala, my mum loved you, and she still does; give her time to come around, okay?"

"I keep thinking, what if? This could have been my life, Tseye. I didn't know how much I missed this until I came here today. Seeing your parents reminded me of how much love is in this house." She turned to smile at him. "You are so lucky, Tseye."

"Zala, this could still be your life. This time, it's for keeps, okay? You have nothing to worry about. Trust me, babe."

* * *

Tseye squeezed Zala's hands, stroking her palm.

He had watched her all evening, knowing she was nervous even though his Mum had smiled and hugged her when they had walked into the house.

"I'm happy for Zuri; she is so excited."

"She already has them wrapped around her little finger." Tseye grinned, nodding towards his parents.

His mother bent to whisper something to Zuri, who burst out laughing before she ran across the room to say excitedly to her mother.

"Grandma said you and I can teach her how to make waffles!"

Zala laughed, ruffling her daughter's hair. "That's nice; I would love to teach her; we could also teach her how to make caramel syrup."

"Yes!" her daughter squealed, racing across the room back to her grandmother, who was laughing.

Tseye turned just as Zala looked across the room and mouthed a thank you to his mother, who nodded and smiled at her.

At that moment, Tseye felt gratitude towards his mother. Oh, she was still angry, but she was willing to let bygones be bygones. All he had to do was convince Zala to let her guard down and feel the love around her.

Raising her hand to his, he kissed the back of her hand, his heart skipping as she smiled at him. It was the first genuine smile he had seen all evening.

* * *

When he returned home to his parents' house after taking Zala and Zuri home, his mother was waiting for him.

"Hey, Mum."

"Tseye." His mother patted the space next to her on the sofa; she waited for her son to sit beside her, then asked quietly, "Is Zala okay? I could tell she was uncomfortable all evening."

"She was worried about meeting you and Dad again."

His mother sighed. "Tseye, as a mother, I am a bit upset that she is back in your life, but that's only because you were devastated when she left you. But if Zala is the person you want to be with, I will always support you. Your father and I both. Tseye, you have to be sure that this is what you want."

"I love her, Mum, and this is for keeps. I promise."

"And Zala?"

Tseye sighed, shaking his head.

"I'm not sure, Mum. I know she loves me; I can feel it, but the fear in her is holding her back. Zala has changed Mum; she's become jumpy, nervous, and no longer as confident as she used to be, I am constantly walking on eggshells around her."

"Tseye, did you say or do something to her?"

His eyes widened. "Are you asking me that mum?

Seriously?"

She reached over and patted his hand. "As a mother, I have to ask."

"Mum, you know me better than that." Tseye was offended that his mum could ask him if he said or did something to cause Zala to be nervous around him.

"Hey, I'm sorry." His mother grinned at him.

"I know." He paused, then said quietly. "She was in a bad marriage, Mum."

"How bad?" she asked quietly, almost afraid of the answer.

"I saw the scars," he said, his voice quiet. "Horrible scars, Mum."

His mother's face paled.

The color drained from her cheeks as the meaning of what he said sank in.

"Oh no," his mother whispered in horror.

Tseye nodded. "The guy was an asshole, a major one. How

her parents made her marry him out of family obligation is beyond me; he looks like a thug. What kind of parents would do that to their daughter?" he asked pained.

"Don't judge, Tseye; you don't know what other choices they had," his mother cautioned him.

"Would you do that to me? Make me marry someone to further Dad's career at the expense of my happiness?"

His mother was quiet for a while before responding, "Tseye, I can't answer that; as I said, maybe that was their only choice, and you should not judge them for that, especially since you want to marry their daughter. I am guessing you hope this will lead to marriage, right?"

Tseye nodded. "That's the idea."

"That's all that matters; nothing else matters."

"Are you willing to accept her as your daughter-in-law, Mum?"

"Tseye, I am the least of your troubles; you need to get Zala to trust again, and it's not going to be as easy as saying I love you. Are you willing to stand by her?"

Tseye nodded. "You bet I am."

"There you have my answer."

Chapter Sixteen

Tseye was waiting for her after the close of work the following Friday.

"Hey." He leaned over and kissed her lightly. "How was work?"

"Stressful," she replied as she fastened her seat belt, wearing a deep scowl. "I need a lot of rest this weekend."

"Oh, rest was not what I had in mind when I asked you to spend the weekend with me." Tseye laughed as he maneuvered the car out of the parking lot and joined the traffic. "We are supposed to meet up with Eyimofe and Naade for dinner, but I can cancel if you are tired?"

"Please?"

"That's fine; I will call them when we get home." "Thank you." She smiled gratefully. "I need to call my Mum to confirm if she and Zuri got in okay," she explained as she thought of Zuri, who had left for Abuja with her Mum. It had become a ritual. Zuri spent the third weekend of every month in Abuja with her parents and was always eager to go.

"I know. I spoke to your mum and Zuri when they got to Abuja." He glanced at her. "Are you okay?"

"I have a slight headache coming on," she replied. "Close your eyes, Zala; I will wake you when we get home."

* * *

Two hours later, Tseye had just finished making dinner when she emerged from the bedroom dressed in one of his T-shirts.

"Just in time." He looked up. "Dinner is ready. Nothing special, just stir-fried noodles." He dished some into a plate and pushed the plate across to her. "Dig in, how are you feeling?"

"Much better. I needed that nap," she replied, taking the fork, he had given her and beginning to eat. I hope Eyimofe and Naade were not too disappointed," she asked.

"No, they understood."

"They still haven't met Zuri, and I haven't met your sister. I feel guilty for blowing them off."

Tseye looked up, pointing a spoon at her.

"Next week, we will hang out with the guys and Yahimba; no excuses again, Zala."

She laughed. "I promise, no excuses."

"Have you given any thought to attending my parents' anniversary party? My Mum invited you and your parents," Tseye asked as he poured her a drink and handed it to her.

She took the glass he offered and drank from it. "Yes, my parents and I will be there."

"Good." He blew her a kiss as he settled down opposite her to eat.

After dinner, he sent her off to the living room, despite her protests and tidied the kitchen.

She was lying on a sheepskin rug watching a movie when he emerged from the kitchen thirty minutes later.

Closing the door behind him, he turned off the lights and walked across the living room to join her.

"Move over," he said, getting on the floor beside her.

She obliged, scooting over, gasping as he gathered her into his arms and rolled her beneath him.

"Hey," she laughed. "What are you doing?"

She wriggled as he tickled her, laughing as he held her hands above her head.

"I haven't gotten my kiss," he said, looking down at her with a grin.

Her face lit up in a beautiful smile, and his breath caught in his throat.

Damn, but she was beautiful.

"A kiss, you say?" she teased.

"Yes, a kiss.," he responded.

"Just a kiss?" she asked again

"We'll see about that; the night is still young, babe."

Releasing her arms, he bent and kissed the scar on her eyelid, then kissed her nose as her arms slid around his neck.

Her touch always excited him.

"I'm still waiting for the kiss," she whispered against his neck before turning to face him.

Needing no further invitation, he bent his head and kissed her, almost coming undone as her mouth opened beneath his, her tongue mating with his, inviting him to taste her.

She always tasted so good; he loved kissing her.

Grasping her neck with one hand, he kissed her again and again until she was clutching at his shirt, her hands sliding beneath to touch the hard planes of his stomach.

Breaking the kiss, he whispered against her mouth. "Zala."

"Hmm," she whispered. "Make love to me, Tseye, don't

stop."

He kissed her eyes as his hands slid down to grip her waist, pushing into her so that she threw her head back, her mouth opening with a soft gasp as he bent and kissed her neck.

"Please, Tseye!" she groaned as his hands grazed under her breast lightly.

"We have all night, Zala," Tseye whispered as he kissed her again, his hands sliding beneath the t-shirt she wore to touch her, before he took it off and got rid of his own shirt.

"Zala." He kissed her again, delighting in her moans from his touch.

She slid her arms around his neck, pulling him down to kiss him again. Rolling, so that she was on top of him, Tseye gave her what she asked for and what he wanted. He made love to her again and again, worshipping her, loving her with his hands, his mouth and his words.

* * *

"I love you, Zala," Tseye whispered later.

She was lying in his arms.

Her eyes filled with tears at his words as she struggled to say something.

"You don't have to say anything, Zala. I want you to know I love you and I will always be here for you."

The tears came then as he settled against her, saying nothing.

She waited until she was sure he was asleep, and then she let the tears fall.

She cried because she knew she could never give him what he wanted.

She could never give him the forever he wanted and deserved.

She was damaged goods; how could anyone want to be with her?

Sometime during the night, Tseye had carried her to the bedroom and placed her in his bed, but he wasn't in bed when she woke up.

Sitting up, she winced as her head started pounding; well, what did she expect? She had cried all through the night. Swinging her legs over the bed, she slid her feet into the slippers by the bed and went to find Tseye. He was standing by the windows in the living room, looking out, hands in the pockets of his shorts.

"Tseye."

He turned at her voice, the corners of his mouth lifting in a slight smile.

"Hey," he greeted her, coming to stand before her.

"Why didn't you wake me?" she asked.

"You needed the sleep," he replied.

"Huh?"

Taking a deep breath, his eyes never leaving hers, he asked quietly, "Why were you crying last night, Zala? Did I hurt you?"

* * *

"No, Tseye, you did not."

Sighing in relief, he asked, "So why were you crying?"

"You said you loved me," she said.

"What?" he asked confused.

"You said you loved me, Tseye." She repeated.

"And that made you cry?"

She nodded.

"I wasn't lying, Zala; I have never hidden how I felt from you, have I?"

"No."

"So why the tears then?" Tseye asked.

Taking a deep breath, she stepped back and said simply, "You can't love me, Tseye."

"Excuse me?" asked Tseye, blinking in surprise as she turned away from him and started walking back towards the bedroom, "Zala, please don't walk away; what do you mean by saying I can't love you?"

She stopped, and without turning to look at him, she said, "Let's just continue with this thing between us; love doesn't have to come into our relationship. Sex between us is good. Why would you want to spoil it with love?"

Tseye couldn't believe what she had just said. He wasn't sure he had heard her right. He asked her again to be sure and almost lost it when she repeated her answer. Walking towards her, he gripped her arm, swinging her around to face him.

"Zala," he began, but she swung at him, hitting his hands as she screamed,

"Let go of me! Don't touch me!"

Her scream caused him to loosen his grip on her arms; raising his hands, he took a step back as she began rubbing her arms furiously.

"Hey, I'm sorry. I'm going to take a step back, and then we can talk, okay?" he said.

"Don't ever touch me again like that, Tseye!"

* * *

Her heart was pounding with fear. She felt like throwing up.

"I am sorry; I didn't mean to scare you," Tseye explained,

keeping his distance away from her till he was sure she was calm enough to let him close.

"Don't touch me like that again," her voice broke and tears fell. "That was how he used to grab me before he hit me."

"I am sorry, Zala, I had no idea"

Zala heard the hurt in his voice, but she was too busy feeling pitiful to care.

"This shouldn't have happened; this thing between us is a mistake; we should never have gotten involved again."

She turned to face Tseye, her eyes devoid of emotion.

"What are you talking about, Zala?"

"I can't give you what you want, Tseye!"

"What do you think I want from you, Zala?"

"You said you loved me; I can't give you a happy ever after; all I can give you is sex!"

"Zala," Tseye began, but she held up her hand, the tears spilling over

"Don't come any closer to me."

"Zala, please, listen to me," Tseye pleaded.

"No, you listen! If we are going to continue, then we have to agree that we are in it just for the sex and nothing else, not happily ever after, no families, no marriage, nothing like that; if you don't agree, then we call it quits, Tseye!"

"Why Zala? A few days ago, at my parent's house, you said you wanted it all, that you could have had it all; what changed between now and then?'

"I came to my senses!"

"What on earth are you talking about?"

Zara shook her head slowly.

"I can't do the marriage thing again. You want love and marriage, don't you?" she asked, her voice almost mechanical, as if it had been rehearsed in her mind for far too long.

Tseye swallowed the lump in his throat, his voice catching. "Yes, I do, Zala. I want you to love me and I want us to get married at some point. I want a family, with you, Zala."

Her bitter laugh hit him like a slap to the face.

"You want that with me? Then we are over, Tseye. Because that is never going to happen." She shook her head as if the idea itself was laughable. "I'm broken, and I can't give you what you want. I can't be the woman you deserve."

* * *

How had this happened? From last night to this.

Tseye stood watching her as she ripped his heart out with each word she spoke.

He felt the pain; her words stung; it felt like she was twisting a knife in his chest. It took all of his self-control to stop himself from reaching for her and shaking her hard.

Instead, he asked quietly, his eyes full of pain. Tseye's chest tightened.

"Why, Zala?"

His voice was barely a whisper, filled with so much hurt that it felt as though its weight could crush him at any moment. "Why is it so impossible for you to believe in us? What happened to the woman I knew? The woman who told me she wanted it all? The woman who wanted a future, a family?"

She sniffed, rubbing her eyes, but he remained silent because he was unsure how she would react if he touched her. She was already on edge, and he needed to get through to her to get her to relax so they could talk like mature adults. He hated confrontations; he always walked away from them, but he couldn't walk away from this one because he knew that if he did, she would never allow him back into her life.

"Why can't you believe in us, Zala?"

"Because I am damaged goods, Tseye."

"Not to me, Zala" his reply was instant, but she shook her head slowly. "Not to me, Zala," he said firmly.

He couldn't bear to see her so lost, so alone, and still, the fear in her eyes, the way she held herself back from him, made him want to scream. "You're not damaged. You are strong, Zala. I can't fix everything, but I'm not going anywhere. I won't hurt you. I could never hurt you."

"I am sorry, Tseye, but I will never get married again, and I can't do that to you, knowing you want marriage."

"Why is the thought of marriage so scary, Zala?"

"I hate the idea of marriage, Tseye; I can't give you what you want; you can't love me; I am damaged, not good enough."

"Is it because of your scars, Zala? You know that does not matter to me."

"It's not because of that!"

"Then what is it, Zala? Please talk to me."

"I can't have kids, okay! I can't! Months after I had Zuri, I was back in the hospital because Negasi hit me, hit me, kicked me in the stomach! I was told I may never be able to have kids! There, I have said it! You made me say it. Are you happy now?" she shouted at him. "And you will want it all, marriage, kids and when I can't give you what you want, you will hit me as Negasi did! Negasi hit me when I couldn't give him what he wanted! I stopped responding to his lovemaking, and he turned on me and began hitting me."

Shocked by her outburst and revelation, Tseye stepped

towards her. His eyes narrowed when she moved from him to stand behind the sofa, which she used as a barrier between them.

She was scared of him, and he could sense it in how she held herself.

His heart broke.

What had Negasi done to her? Forcing himself to a stop, he slid his hands into the pockets of his shorts.

"I'm not him," he repeated softly. "I'm not going to hurt you; I would never do anything to hurt you. And I won't force you to be something you're not. I'm not asking you to have kids or get married if you don't want that. But I want you. I've always wanted you, Zala."

He watched, aware she was shutting and tuning him out, and he didn't want that.

"How can you say that after everything I've told you?" she whispered. "How can you still want me after what I've been through?"

Tseye closed the space between them gently, cautiously, stopping when she moved back from him, even though the sofa was between them. He needed her to feel safe with him again.

"Because I love you. Because despite everything, you're the woman I've always loved."

She looked away from him, and Tseye's heart ached for her. She wasn't listening. He struggled to hold back the tears that threatened to fall. How could she have become so broken and not believe in herself? When she turned back to look at him, her stare was blank.

"Take me home, Tseye."

Chapter Seventeen

He took her home.

She hadn't said a word to him the entire drive back, and he let her be, knowing that if he spoke to her, she would push him away.

And he didn't want that.

She turned to face him when he parked outside her house.

"I'm sorry, Tseye, I can't do this again; I can't do this to you; you deserve better."

"Zala, don't do this."

She shook her head slowly, pulling further away.

"No, I shouldn't have gotten involved with you again." She looked away from him, her teeth worrying her bottom lip, "But I am not going to stop you from seeing Zuri."

"Really?" Tseye asked, gripping the steering wheel hard as he looked at her. "How will that work, Zala? How do I deal with you?"

"We are grown-ups; we can handle this."

"Don't do that, Zala, don't belittle what we have," Tseye warned, looking away from her, his mouth tightening in anger.

She shook her head. "I am so sorry Tseye" "Can you stop apologizing, and let's talk?"

She shook her head slowly as she reached for the door.

"We have nothing to say to each other; please don't make this hard for me."

"Hard for you?" Tseye rasped. "You think this isn't hard on me?"

"I am sorry, Tseye," she said again as she exited the car, heaving a sigh of relief as he made no effort to touch or prevent her from leaving.

He had no idea how hard this was for her; she was okay with the relationship the way it was; why did he have to go and bring up love?

Marriage was not for her, and if she didn't make that clear now, it would be harder for both of them; she couldn't do it to Tseye; he deserved so much more.

Just as she was about to close the door, he said quietly, "I am not going to give up on us, Zala."

She said nothing but turned and walked into the compound, holding back her tears.

She knew he was waiting for her to enter the house before driving off.

Zala unlocked the door, dropping her weekend bag on the floor in the living room before she collapsed on the sofa, and burst into tears.

* * *

He had come straight from Zala to Eyimofe's house to meet Eyimofe and Naade, lamenting over the women in their lives.

"Are you going to call Yahimba?" he asked Eyimofe, who was packing his bags in readiness for his trip to London.

He shook his head. "No, there's no point; she made it clear she wants nothing to do with me," his friend replied.

"So, you are just going to give up on her like that?" Naade asked as he tossed a handful of nuts into his mouth.

Eyimofe turned to look at them. "What do you guys want me to do? I have called and sent messages. Hell, I spent the last week camped outside her apartment and she still wouldn't let me inside. There is only so much a man can take before giving up, and I dare say I have done my best. She wants out of our relationship, and that's fine. It's like she was always waiting for me to fail. She finally has what she wants."

Tseye said nothing, Yahimba was like Zala, who had compared him to her ex, Negasi but still Yahimba was his sister, and he wasn't going to sit back and let her destroy what she had with Eyimofe, who was planning to travel without her after putting him through hell to get her passport sorted out.

"And, of course, a trip to London is the next best thing," Tseye hissed. "You were going to take my sister with you, you moron."

He knew he sounded like a jerk, but he was angry.

After his parents' anniversary party, he would take a trip to London; thinking of his parents' anniversary party, he turned to Eyimofe and asked, "You will be back in time for that, right, my parents' anniversary party?"

"You know I wouldn't miss it," his friend replied, zipping his suitcase shut.

"I think you should call Yahimba before you leave, at least," Tseye said quietly.

"Tseye, you've been moody since you came in. Are you okay?" asked Naade.

Tseye scoffed.

How would they react to the news that he and Zala had called it quits again?

His friends would blame him for getting involved with her

again.

"She called it off."

"Who?" asked Eyimofe, who had turned to leave the room.

"Zala, she broke up with me."

There was silence, and then Eyimofe returned to the living room and sat down as Naade sat up in his chair.

"What happened?" Naade asked. "I thought you said things were going well?"

"Aren't you going to say I told you so?" Tseye responded to Naade's question with a question.

"You know that's not how we deal with stuff, Tseye," Eyimofe replied, raising his eyebrow.

"You warned me, guys; maybe I should have listened."

"You said everything was going so well between you two, even though you haven't introduced us to Zuri yet," Eyimofe remarked. "So, what happened?"

"I told her I loved her." Tseye's voice was full of pain as he responded to Eyimofe's question.

"How is that an issue? Isn't that what ladies want to hear?" asked Naade, smirking when Eyimofe glared at him.

"Not Zala; she wants to be in a no-strings relationship; marriage is not on the cards for her,"

Tseye muttered.

"She said that?" Naade asked.

Tseye nodded, rubbing his forehead. "She said that and much more, and I don't care to repeat what she said."

"You don't need to. What did you do, say to her?" Eyimofe asked.

"I don't know what to do or what else to say to convince her of how I feel about her," he admitted, his voice raw with the weight of his own pain. "She's shutting me out, and I don't know how to get through to her. She thinks she's broken. She thinks that because of her past, because of what Negasi did to her, she's damaged, and she doesn't deserve anything better. I've tried to tell her that's untrue, but she can't hear me."

Eyimofe, who had been quietly listening, leaned for- ward with a thoughtful expression. "You need to give her time, Tseye. Healing doesn't happen overnight. And she won't let you in if she feels like you're pushing her into a box she's not ready for."

Naade nodded. "Eyimofe is right; it is going to take time for her to get over the horror of her first marriage, especially one that left scars."

Leaning back against his seat, Tseye closed his eyes, swallowing hard.

"Tseye?" Eyimofe touched him lightly on the knee.

"She may not be able to have kids; he hit her, and the result is that she may not be able to have any more children; she says she is damaged goods," Tseye explained.

"What the hell? Who is this guy?" Naade demanded, jumping up.

"A monster, that's what he is; where is Zala?" Eyimofe's eyes filled with horror at what Tseye had just said about Zala.

"I dropped her off at home; why?"

"Sometimes," Naade said, his tone a little softer, "the best way to show someone you care is to give them room to breathe."

Tseye nodded.

The conversation hung in the air, leaving Tseye with more questions than answers.

How could he convince Zala that she wasn't broken? How could he show her he would never hurt her like Negasi? Maybe Naade was right; maybe he needed to give her space to breathe, but that scared him.

How could he give her the space she needed without completely losing her?

* * *

Two weeks later, Zala still wasn't answering his calls.

He hadn't seen her since she said they should end their relationship.

When he showed up to pick up Zuri, the nanny was always available to hand his daughter over to him.

Tseye was not the patient kind, and he was losing it.

Only the thought of pushing her away held him back from confronting her. He had to make her see; she was wrong about what they had.

He wasn't Negasi; how could she think he would hurt her?

"Hi." He smiled as the nanny opened the door and handed him his daughter's weekend bag.

"Good afternoon, Sir." The nanny curtsied as she held the door open for him.

Usually, he would come in and wait for Zuri inside the foyer, but today, he wouldn't do that. What was the point? Zala wouldn't come out to see him anyway.

"Can you bring Zuri to the car when she is ready to leave? I am parked on the driveway."

The air felt heavier around him as he walked out of the house and stood by the car, leaning against it as he waited for Zuri to appear. The faint hum of traffic seemed to fade into the background as his mind circled back to Zala's words.

I can't have kids. I'm damaged. She has told him.

And the truth was that he wanted more kids with her.

* * *

Zala stood by the window, watching as Tseye strapped his daughter into the car seat before getting into the car and reversing out of the compound.

So, he hadn't bothered to come into the house today to wait for Zuri. And he hadn't asked after her like he always did. That hurt, it hurt a lot.

"How long are you going to avoid him?" her mother asked, her expression sad. "And why are you watching him from the window?"

Zala sighed and turned away. "I wasn't watching him, Mum."

"You could have fooled me!" her mother snapped, eye- ing her as she sat down. "Why are you doing this, Zala?"

"It's for his good, Mum. I can't give him the happily ever after he wants; what if he wants more kids? I can't have kids, Mum."

"The word was may; the doctor said you may not have kids; wasn't that what you said? And did you give Tseye a chance to digest this news and react before you called it off and walked away from him for the second time?" her mother asked.

"What's there to digest, Mum? Tseye may be okay with it,

but what about his parents, Mum?"

"Are you in a relationship with his parents, Zala?"

"This is Nigeria, Mum; you are in a relationship with his whole family!" Zala mumbled, shaking her head.

"Ah, Zala." Her mum sighed. "You were with this guy for how long again? Three years? Four years? You married someone else, divorced and still returned to the same guy again. Lucky for you, he is still single and wants to be with you," her mother said. "Tseye is not Negasi."

"I know that, Mum."

"So, what are you doing then? If you know that, why are you doing this?" her mother's voice was full of despair.

"Marriage is not for me! I don't want to be tied down to any man who can turn on me anytime, and that can happen as long as he is a man, that can happen." Zala looked at her mother, eyes wide.

Her mother was quiet for a moment then she shook her head.

"I know you've been through a lot; I wish you would let go and open up, speak to me, anyone, about what you went through because this is ruining your life, and you are being very unfair to Tseye."

"Mum!"

"It's true! Has he ever been abusive? Zala, Negasi is the

one who deserves all your hate. Speaking of Negasi, have you decided what to do about him and his custody battle? Your dad called to let us know he accompanied his parents to Nigeria and is coming here tomorrow to see Zuri; you haven't said anything about that. Was that why you allowed Tseye to take Zuri away for the weekend?"

"Yes!" Zala turned. "I have no intention of letting him see Zuri; I am still upset that he is coming to this house to see me. I am so angry that you allowed it!"

"Oh, I allowed it alright because I need to see that bastard so I can give him a few slaps."

Zala smiled. "Mum, Dad already did that!"

"He didn't do enough," her mother retorted. "And you have to face him; it's the first step to healing after what you have been through."

"After I confront him, what next?"

"Zala, I am not asking you to do this for Tseye; whatever you decide, your dad and I will stand by you; you need to do this for yourself; healing starts from within you."

Her mother was right.

Zala turned to look out at the garden, squinting.

Her mother was right; she needed to deal with Negasi once and for all.

She blinked as tears filled her eyes; she missed Tseye.

She missed him so much that it hurt, but she couldn't give him what he wanted.

When he told her he loved her, she broke down in tears because she knew that marriage was on the cards for him, and she was done with marriage.

Negasi had ruined that for her, and she would never remarry.

Her marriage had been horrible; she shuddered as she recalled everything she had gone through.

Glancing down at her ring finger, she shook her head; a wedding ring for her was a sign that she was in prison.

A prison she could not escape from if she went in again.

Chapter Eighteen

Zala was nervous about an upcoming meeting for the second time in recent weeks.

The first time was when she had to meet Tseye's parents and introduce them to Zuri.

This time, she was waiting for Negasi.

She glanced at the documents he'd had delivered to the Ethiopian Embassy in Abuja, documents from the family courts back home in Addis Ababa summoning her for a custody hearing.

She couldn't believe he had the nerve to do this, knowing that Zuri was not really his daughter.

She was standing by the window, looking out, when she saw the massive gates swing open to allow a black SUV through.

The vehicle stopped next to her car, and the door opened and Negasi got out.

She hadn't seen her ex-husband in months, seeing him now, reminded her of how sick she always felt whenever he tried to touch her.

How had she stayed married to this man?

Negasi Abebe was slightly shorter than she was and burly in stature. With his broad forehead and thick fleshy lips, she had never considered him good-looking. The only thing he had going for him was that he was from a wealthy and prominent family, which meant nothing to her, as she was also from a wealthy family.

She watched as he disappeared into the house and turned to face the door, waiting for him to appear.

It was show time.

Negasi walked in, face scowling.

He always looked angry anyway; nothing new.

"Where is my daughter?" he bellowed. "You made me come over here to see my daughter after taking her out of the country without my permission."

"You permitted her to travel," Zala reminded him.

"You have another custody hearing which you must attend."

"That custody hearing will not happen; Negasi, why are you here?" She remained calm, not allowing him to see how scared she was.

"Are you stupid?" he spat at her. "I have come to see my daughter."

Zala took a deep breath, shocked to realize she was calm instead of trembling as usual when he became angry.

Too calm, she realised. "Zuri isn't here, Negasi."

"Then where is she? Why isn't she here to see me when I told you I would visit today?"

"Zuri is at her grandparent's house; she is spending the weekend with her father, Tseye and his family."

There, it was finally out.

She watched, fascinated as the muscles in Negasi's forehead bulged, indicating he was ready to explode.

Some things never change.

"What did you say?" he bellowed, causing her to wince as his voice vibrated through the house.

Thank goodness Zuri wasn't home.

"You heard me very well; Zuri is with her father. Remember him, my ex, Tseye."

"Call him and ask him to bring my daughter back here."

Call him.

Call who?

Tseye?

She smiled. Oh, how she would love to, but no, she had to do this herself. She had to deal with Negasi herself.

She stepped towards him and almost laughed at the surprise in his eyes.

"Why would I call him? I just told you; she is with her father," she said.

"You don't want to go down that road, Zala; I can destroy you and your family with a snap of my fingers," Negasi said, snapping his fingers in her face. "Your family depends on my family's goodwill; all I have to do is let certain people know that you cheated on me during our marriage, and you and your family are done."

Was he threatening her?

Did he realize he had no power over her or her daughter here in Nigeria?

"I am no longer your wife, Negasi. You can't order me around anymore and let me make it clear: you can't touch me anymore."

Negasi snorted, coming round to take a seat.

He crossed his legs and looked up at her with a smirk. "I can see that you have grown a pair of wings; you can now talk back to me, which is why I want my daughter with me, so she doesn't learn these behaviors from you," he snapped at her. "Call that man and ask him to bring Zuri home."

"No, I will do no such thing."

"Haven't you heard a word I said, Zala? Don't test me; I am running out of patience."

"I heard you," Zala snorted, walking back toward the window. She looked out at the busy road for a moment before turning back to look at him. Now you listen to me. You will get up and leave this house and forget that Zuri and I exist."

"What?" Negasi spat.

"You have a nerve, walking into my parent's house and demanding that I hand my daughter over to you. After all you put me through, you walk in here and threaten to ruin my family. How dare you?" Zala shouted. "How dare you?"

"Did you not hear a word I said? I can ruin you and your family!" he snapped at her.

"Go ahead, then watch me release all my doctor's reports, providing proof of how I was your punching bag for years. Oh, I forgot, your mother runs an organization supporting victims of domestic violence, doesn't she? And yet her beloved son was abusing his wife, physically and verbally!" Zara retorted; she could not believe he was sitting here throwing threats around.

Was he insane?

Negasi shot up to his feet, bristling with anger. "You wouldn't dare!"

"Oh, I would, Negasi. It will be payback for the hell you put me through, and I will reveal that Zuri is not your child, you impotent bastard! Three years plus with me, and you couldn't even get me pregnant, yet you are here demanding I hand over another man's child to you!"

He took a threatening step towards her, his hands raised as though he was about to hit her, but she stood her ground, even though she was terrified.

"You bitch! How dare you talk back to me?" he shouted, grabbing her hands and squeezing it hard, pulling her so she stumbled towards him.

"I will give you five minutes to let go of me, Negasi," she said softly, her eyes filled with disgust.

Maybe it was the tone of her voice or the look in her eyes that made him drop her hands and take a step back.

Zala looked down at where he had gripped her and saw red.

Even here in Nigeria, he was trying to manhandle her, trying to hurt her.

Hadn't he done enough?

"How dare you put your filthy hands on me?" she asked,

rubbing the spot where he had gripped her.

"I will do much more than that if you continue this!"

"You will do no such thing!" Zala spat at him, standing close to him, hands on her waist as she faced up to him. "What else can you do except hit me? The difference is that this is Nigeria, not Addis Ababa, and you won't get away with laying a finger on me. Look around you, Negasi; my people, not yours, surround me. One word from me, and you will be beaten to a pulp, and nothing, I repeat, nothing will happen! So, what is it going to be? Do I get them to throw you out, or will you walk out of here on your own?"

"You would keep Zuri away from my parents simply because we are divorced? How vindictive can you be, Zala?" Negasi asked, swallowing hard as he realised he was losing the battle.

"You do realize Zuri is not your child, and she has met her father? What reason do I give him when I allow Zuri to visit you and your parents?" Zala asked him.

"You are sleeping with him, aren't you?" His question surprised her, and she blinked, wondering how the conversation had taken this turn.

He was delusional if he thought he had the right to question her.

It was time he left before things escalated; she moved, walking away to stand behind a sofa.

"I don't see how that is your business, Negasi."

"I was right! You were sleeping with him while still married to me! I knew it; how long were you seeing him behind my back? How long, Zala? I knew you were cheating on me, I could sense it, which was why you ran here to Lagos as soon as we got divorced to be with him!"

"If that is the story you will run with, feel free to expose me. It's time you left Negasi. We are done here. Zuri and I are dead to you! I have already instructed my lawyers in Addis Ababa to submit my documents informing the judge that Zuri is not your child; copies of the DNA results you had carried out will also be submitted so you have no claim to Zuri. If I am going to be painted as a cheating ex-wife to get rid of you, so be it!"

Zala shook her head in disgust, at the fact that he believed she had cheated on him with Tseye. She stood watching as he struggled to control his temper.

Her threat of him getting beaten up had scared him; she had seen the fear in his eyes when she made that threat.

The bloody coward, he couldn't even call her bluff.

"This is not over!"

"As far as I am concerned, it is; now please leave Negasi."

"I will make sure everybody knows how you cheated on me during our marriage," he repeated, shaking his thick fist at her; then he turned around and stormed out of the

don't know?"

His mother shrugged.

"Speaking of Yahimba, is she coming to the anniversary party?" he asked.

She shrugged. "I don't know, she returned the invitation your dad sent to her."

* * *

Why are women full of so much drama?

Tseye wondered as he was shown to Yahimba's office.

He saw the surprise on her face when he walked in, she hadn't been expecting him, he realised.

"Tseye," she said, getting to her feet.

"Hi, I stopped by to drop off the invite to our parent's anniversary party," Tseye explained, as he dropped a white envelope, embossed with gold lettering, onto the table.

"I don't think your mother would want me there," she said quietly, her gaze dropping as she handed the envelope back to him.

"You think? She asked me to drop this off with you; you are family, Yahimba, you know that."

He couldn't understand what was going through his

sister's head. They were reaching out to her, and all she had to do was accept their offer of friendship.

But no, she had to be stubborn like Zala.

Like Zala, who had refused to take his calls or even agree to a meeting, how could someone be so insensitive and not care how her actions would affect others?

Could she not see that Zuri would start asking questions soon?

First, he would deal with Yahimba and then visit Zala. "I'm sorry, but I'd rather not attend.," his sister replied. Tseye got up, a sad smile on his face.

He wished she would stop being stubborn and give his parents a chance.

"Yahimba, you do yourself no favors shutting yourself off from the world. You have so much love to give and receive if you give yourself a chance." He held up a hand when she opened her mouth to speak. "I'm going to leave now, but I'm going to say one thing to you, and I am not saying it because Eyimofe is one of my best friends. Eyimofe is an amazing human being, a decent guy, and he would never do what you suspect him of. He's given you all he's got and tried to make up with you. Pardon me for saying this, but you are so thick-headed you can't see past your issues to recognize a good man. I hope you don't regret your decision because I know for sure that Eyimofe is done." He paused, then said quietly, "My folks and I have done everything within our power to make you feel at home, especially my mother and she does not need to. Let's face it: you feel you will always be the child of the woman my father had an affair with, so what? My mother and I do not care about that; you are and will always be family. Our home is always open to you, though. If you want a relationship with my parents and me, we are always waiting."

Glad that he had said what he had to say, he leaned forward, dropped the card on the table before her and turned around to leave her office.

Chapter Nineteen

After three weeks in Abuja, she was ready to return to Lagos.

Abuja had been a nice break from Lagos.

She made the impulsive decision to move there when she could no longer avoid Tseye's calls.

Volunteering to oversee a project in Abuja, she left a message for Tseye informing him of her trip. She told herself that she was doing it to keep him informed of Zuri's itinerary, but the truth was that she missed him.

The following Monday, she left for Abuja for work, taking Zuri with her after informing Tseye she would return in three weeks.

His reply had been short; that's fine, he'd texted back.

She glanced at her watch as she wheeled her suitcase through the arrival hall toward the parking lot, where her driver was waiting to pick her up.

Zuri had returned a week ago with her mother to resume school.

Minutes later, she had located her driver and was soon on her way towards Ikoyi.

Her phone rang as soon she got home.

Glancing down, she saw that it was Lola calling. "Hey," she answered on the third ring.

"Are you back?" Lola asked without mincing words.

"I just got in," she replied.

"Are you going to Tseye's parent's anniversary party?"

Was she?

"I am not sure yet; I just got in from Abuja."

"You should go. I ran into Tseye and Naade and got an invite; I am going, and you are coming with me. I'll pick you up at 7 p.m., so you better be ready. I spoke to your Mum, and she said Tseye picked Zuri up to get her hair done," Lola said.

Zuri nodded. "Yes, Tseye texted me to let me know; his Mum was going to take Zuri to get her hair done and try out her outfit."

"Perfect, see you at 7 pm."

* * *

She wasn't sure if this was the right outfit for Tseye's parents' anniversary party.

She stood in front of the mirror, eyes scanning her reflection.

Her dark green gown shimmered under the light, its rich satin fabric catching every subtle shift in movement. The bodice hugged her frame like a second skin, clinched at the waist with a delicate brooch that added understated glamour.

From there, the gown cascaded to the floor in fluid folds, its elegant sweep almost ethereal. Reaching up, her fingers brushed against the delicate neckline, adjusting it slightly. The subtle plunge framed her collarbones, and the elegant and demure curve was a perfect balance of allure and sophistication.

Turning, she glanced over her shoulder.

Was this truly the right outfit for the occasion?

Tseye had bought it for her on their last trip to Dubai, and he had wanted to see her in it.

Well, tonight, he would.

This was the perfect event to wear this outfit too.

Slipping her feet into dark gold slippers, she took a deep breath. She looked beautiful. She knew that, but she was also very nervous.

Tonight, after weeks of avoiding him, she was going to face Tseye but had no idea what she would say to him.

But one thing she was sure of was she had missed him. Part of her wanted to call up and say she couldn't attend, but then she wondered what she would tell her daughter Zuri, who had begun asking why they never hung out as a family anymore.

* * *

The party was being held at Civic Hall, Victoria Island. The moment she walked in, Zala tensed up and became nervous. Clutching her purse, she stopped walking and turned to face Lola.

"I need some air, Lola. I will join you in a couple of minutes."

"Are you okay?"

"Yes, I am; give me a minute." She turned and left the hall.

Walking outside, she hurried to the one of the cars parked across and leaned against the first car she came across, her heart beating fast.

She could do it.

She was Zala Kebede, brave, strong and confident.

She could face Tseye and behave like the mature woman she was. She would tell him, she missed him and although she was scared, she wanted to be with him, yes, she could do it.

Closing her eyes, she began to count to ten when she heard a sound behind her.

"Zala," Tseye said.

* * *

Tseye was standing with Misan and Naade when Zala walked in.

He had just turned to take a drink from the waiter standing by him when he saw her and his breath caught in his throat as he took her in.

He had bought that dress for her on their last trip to Dubai, and God knew he had imagined her wearing it many times.

She looked gorgeous.

As she moved, the gown seemed to move with her, swaying softly around her hips, a perfect balance of grace and boldness.

His eyes narrowed as she stopped and whispered something to Lola before she turned and left the hall.

Why was she leaving?

There was no way he would let her leave tonight, until he had spoken to her.

"Guys, give me a moment, please."

Misan, who was still miffed at Eyimofe for not allowing her to stay and listen to his conversation with Yahimba, nodded.

Walking briskly, he followed Zala out of the hall.

When he emerged from the hall, his gaze locked on her instantly.

She stood with her back to him, leaning against one of the sleek cars parked near the entrance. Although her posture was casual, something about the way she held herself made him hesitate.

He ached to bridge the distance between them, to reach out and touch her, but the impulse was quickly swallowed by a flood of restraint. Instead, he slid his hands into his pants pockets, fingers curling around the fabric as though grounding himself.

"Zala," he murmured.

At the sound of her name, he felt her freeze. Every muscle in her body went taut, and he felt it: the sharp shift in the air, the sudden tension between them.

"Tseye…" She turned to face him, her throat tightening as their gazes locked. The moment stretched between them, both fragile and intense. Her voice trembled slightly, though she tried to mask it with a smile.

"You came," he said softly.

She hesitated, unsure of what to say.

"Are you okay?" he asked moving towards her.

She nodded but still didn't speak.

Tseye nodded too, his heart racing, he was sure hers was racing too.

He didn't push her for an answer. Instead, his eyes searched hers, concern lingering on his features.

"Why are you outside, Zala? I saw you come in with Lola, and... you look beautiful."

"Thank you," she whispered, barely breathing.

His steady and searching gaze never left hers. "Why are you outside?" the question came again, this time more insistent. The silence thickened, and he felt himself falling into her stare.

"I was nervous." The words escaped her before she could stop them, soft and raw.

"You don't need to be," he murmured, his voice low, almost tender.

Without another word, he reached for her hand, his fingers brushing hers with the gentlest of touches. The warmth of his skin sent a shiver through her. "You are here with me."

His words wrapped around her like a promise, and the knot in his chest relaxed.

In that quiet, stolen moment, everything felt right, like they were the only two people in the world.

"You look beautiful. I'm honored to be your date," he said, his voice low, sincere, and full of meaning.

His eyes locked on hers, softening the moment as they both stood there, just a heartbeat away.

She smiled at him, her lips curling, but her eyes had a playful gleam. "Who said I was your date?" she teased, her voice light but with a touch of mischief and, more importantly, relief.

His gaze never faltered.

It was as if the entire world had narrowed down to just the two of them, and nothing else mattered. Slowly and deliberately, he raised her hand to his lips, kissing her knuckles softly, a quiet promise hidden in the gesture.

"Whose date are you then?" he asked.

"Tseye..." she began hesitantly, she tried to pull away from him, but he wasn't letting her.

"Let me go, we are in public, people are looking this way."

He placed a finger gently on her lips, his touch both a request and a command.

"Don't say anything, Zala. Please, you came to my parent's party, just relax, please." His voice softened further, becoming almost a whisper. "But so that you know, you're not going anywhere until we've had that talk."

Her breath hitched, a rush of confusion and longing flooding her all at once.

"Tseye," his name fell from her lips like a prayer.

But he shook his head, his eyes dark with something unreadable, something raw.

Without a word, he pulled her into his arms, his hands sliding around her waist easily as though they had always belonged there.

"God, I've missed you," he whispered, his breath warm against her ear.

Before she could respond, he bent his head and kissed her, slow, lingering, his lips claiming hers in a way that felt like home, like every moment apart had led to this one night.

She melted into him, the world outside fading as the heat between them flared once more.

He held her close, the kiss deepening as though it could undo all the space and time that had kept them apart.

* * *

With her lips still tingling from the pressure of his mouth against hers, Zala followed Tseye back into the hall, the warmth of the kiss lingering like a whisper against her skin.

Every step felt heavier with the echo of that moment, but she pushed it down, focusing on the soft hum of the evening around them.

Tseye had said they would talk.

"Misan is in town," Tseye said, his voice smooth, but there was a quiet undercurrent of something she couldn't place.

He guided her towards Misan and Naade, who stood laughing and chatting with Tseye's mother.

Alero Harriman's face immediately lit up with a warm smile.

"Zala!" she exclaimed, her eyes sparkling. She opened her arms, and Zala found herself enveloped in a warm, welcoming hug. "You made it! Your mum wasn't sure you would," Alero added, her voice full of affection as she pulled away and held Zala at arm's length, inspecting her with a smile. "Thank you for coming."

"I'm glad you came. I am going to join Eyimofe's mum. I will catch up with you all later." Alero smiled at them, as she turned and walked away.

Zala gave a sigh of relief as Tseye squeezed her hand, she hadn't expected this warmth from Tseye's mum. The last time she'd been at the house, Alero Harriman had been polite and welcoming, but she couldn't remember her being this warm.

What had changed, she wondered as she watched Ts- eye's mother walk away.

Turning, she moved to hug Misan and Naade, both of them greeting her with warm embraces. But her thoughts kept flickering back to Tseye.

His touch, his words, the way he'd kissed her like she was all that mattered in that moment. The kiss still burned on her lips, and she couldn't help but wonder if he still felt the same way.

Leaning to whisper in his ear, she said, "I'm going to look for my Mum and Zuri." Tseye nodded, squeezing her hand.

Misan watched Zala walk away, her steps purposeful yet slightly hesitant, before she turned to look at Tseye, her eyes glinting with mischief.

A playful smirk tugged at the corners of her lips, but there was a sharp curiosity beneath it.

"Spill," she said, her tone light but insistent.

"Spill what?" Tseye asked, his voice low, almost guarded.

He couldn't help but notice the way Misan's gaze held his, a challenge that made him feel both on edge and strangely amused.

"Are you guys back together?"

Tseye's response was immediate, though his laughter was forced, a hint of defensiveness creeping in. "I'm not saying anything to you, Misan!" He crossed his arms, the gesture an unconscious shield against her probing.

She raised an eyebrow, unfazed. "Why ever not?"

He sighed, a playful, almost resigned look flashing across his face as he leaned back slightly. "Because you'll tell your mum," He began, his voice lowering as if he were recounting a well-worn script, "who will then tell my mum, and then I'll have to hear about it from my mum, who'll eventually tell my dad at the family dinner."

"Ah! Misan! Wahala be like bicycle," Naade said laughing, "Is that how it is now?"

Misan chuckled at the image Tseye had painted, her eyes dancing with amusement.

"Fair enough," she teased, though there was an edge of something deeper in her tone. "But you know I can't keep a

secret. If something's going on between you two if you are back together, I will know; it's written all over your face."

Tseye shook his head, grinning.

"I swear, Misan, you really know how to make a guy feel exposed."

"Misan, I wonder how Eyimofe survived with you as an

elder sister," Naade chuckled, shaking his head as he gave Misan an exaggerated look of sympathy.

Misan didn't miss a beat.

Tseye chuckled as he watched her, she never ever backed down from a challenge, Naade knew that so why had he said that to Misan?

She turned to Naade, her eyes narrowing with playful warning. "Don't worry, Naade," she said, her voice dripping with sweetness, "I heard about Obehi."

Tseye, who had been quietly observing their banter couldn't help but chuckle at the immediate shift in Naade's expression.

His easy smile faltered, and a scowl replaced it in the blink of an eye.

Talk about killing a guy's groove.

Misan had effortlessly turned the tables, and Naade's good mood evaporated like mist in the sun.

When are you getting married again?" Misan continued, her tone innocent.

Tseye, ever the instigator, leaned in with a grin. "Wedding's set for early next year" he teased, fully aware that he was fanning the flames.

He watched as Naade's scowl deepened.

"I don't believe that Zala," he said, his voice tighten- ing with frustration. "What are you so scared of? Things between us were fine until I said I love you, and then you ran like I'd burned you." His words hung in the air, raw and unguarded, as if he were searching for answers he couldn't quite reach.

When she didn't respond, he took a step forward, closing the distance between them but as she instinctively took a step back, he paused, his eyes narrowing with quiet intensity.

"I'm not going to touch you," he said, his voice low, each word deliberate. "If that's what you're scared of."

His gaze held hers, a mixture of frustration and some- thing more as if he were silently pleading for her to face him and stop running.

It was as though she could feel the weight of his frustration because in that moment, her throat tightened, and suddenly, her eyes brimmed with unshed tears.

The sting was immediate and unbidden, and she quickly blinked them back, but her vulnerability was undeniable; he saw it reflected in her eyes.

"Zala?"

* * *

God, why couldn't Tseye just understand?

She thought, her chest tightening as the weight of her fear pressed down on her.

How could she be with him when she couldn't give him what he deserved?

What if, someday, he wanted more children, children she couldn't give him?

What would happen to her then?

Her voice trembled as the words slipped out. "You would want more, Tseye. More than I can give."

It hurt her to say it, but she had to.

As he stepped closer and his hands found her shoulders, she felt the shift in his energy.

But she didn't pull away.

His relief that she stayed still when he touched her, was almost palpable, and she allowed herself to feel it for a brief, fragile moment. But it only broke her further.

Her heart cracked wide open, guilt flooding in as she realised she had done this to him.

She had made him nervous.

She had made him hesitant around her, unsure of how she would react or handle his touch or words, which hurt.

It hurt because Tseye was an amazing person and didn't

deserve any of this.

"I love you, Tseye," she whispered, her voice crack- ing under the weight of her admission, her vulnerability. "Which is why it's best I stay away from you."

He froze as her words sank in.

His hands tightened on her shoulders, and she felt his intense gaze, searching for something in her face that he didn't find.

"If you love me like you say you do," he pleaded, "then you'll let me in. We'll deal with this shit together. What are you afraid of, Zala? That I'd want kids? We already have Zuri, don't we? And we'll have each other, so what are you so scared of?"

She shook her head, her tears falling freely now. "What if you want more kids?" she whispered.

"What if I don't?" He tilted her face up, his thumb brushing away a tear from her cheek.

Her heart ached as she met his eyes. "What if I don't, Zala?" he repeated, his gaze soft but intense, as though he was trying to convince her with the force of his sincerity.

She could barely hold it together.

Her breath hitched as she forced out the words that had been buried deep. "You might change. Negasi did."

Tseye's grip on her chin tightened ever so slightly, but his voice remained firm. "I am not Negasi, Zala. I love you, and I would never hurt you." His words were soft but filled with an unwavering conviction. "If we can't have kids, we'll adopt as long as you're okay with that; we will adopt. Don't you know that I would never hurt you?"

She swallowed hard, her chest tight with emotion as her tears fell freely.

"I'm scared, Tseye," she whispered. "Of what?"

"Everything." She inhaled shakily, her chest tight, fear- ing what could be. "You'll want to get married. That's the kind of person you are. I've been there before. I've done that, and it was a horrible experience. I don't want to go through that again."

She felt his stare on her face; she looked up, and their eyes met.

He held her gaze, his eyes searching hers as if to absorb every ounce of her pain. Then, slowly, he reached up, his thumb brushing away another tear. "Zala, I'm not going to lie to you." His voice was soft but firm, unwavering in its sincerity. "I do want to marry you. I want to put a ring on your finger and shout to the world that you're mine and only mine. I want to see your stomach swollen with my child; yes, I want all of that. I won't lie to you about that. But hear me now…" He leaned forward, placing a gentle kiss on her cheek before continuing. "I won't mention marriage until you're ready. If and when we get married after I've shown you that marriage can be a wonderful experience... If we decide we want more kids, we'll adopt. But only if you're okay with it."

Her breath hitched again, her chest constricting as the weight of his words settled into her heart.

"Tseye?" she whispered, barely able to speak through the tears.

* * *

"Zala, please don't shut me out," he pleaded. "I've been going crazy since you left me again. I love you, and I'm prepared to wait. All I ask is that you let me in. Trust me." His eyes searched hers, pleading for a glimpse of the woman he knew was still there the woman who loved him.

He reached down and held her face in his hands, so she had no choice but to look at him.

"I love you," he said again, desperate to get to her.

He knew the moment she truly heard him, the moment his declaration of love landed, her eyes shimmered with unshed tears, the weight of her own emotions breaking through the barrier she had built around herself.

"I'm sorry, Tseye," she whispered, her voice breaking as she let the sobs slip free.

His heart ached for her, but he didn't let her pull away. "Don't be," he murmured softly, pulling her closer into his arms.

He held her tightly, feeling the tremble of her body against his as she cried.

The vulnerability in her sobs unraveled him, but he wasn't about to let her push him away again.

Not this time.

"I'm selfish," she said, her words muffled against his chest as she sobbed into him.

"No, Zala," he whispered, his voice thick with emotion, "you're not selfish. You're just scared."

Her pain tightened his chest, but he didn't pull away. He knew she needed this; she needed to cry, to release the storm that had been building inside her.

To release all the pain and hurt, she had trapped within her.

It wasn't going to be easy breaking through the wall surrounding her heart, but he would be there holding her hands until she was ready to take the next step in their relationship.

He had lost her once and wasn't ready to let her go a second time.

He held her, his arms firm and steady, the warmth of his embrace offering her a silent comfort. He didn't say anything; he just let her cry, letting the weight of her emotions fill the space between them.

He wasn't going to rush her.

She needed this release, and he would be there, quietly, without expectation.

Time seemed to stretch; her sobs gradually gave way to softer hiccups.

When she finally pulled back, her eyes red and swollen, he gently cupped her face, brushing away the stray tears still clinging to her cheeks. His voice was soft but laced with concern. "Are you okay?" he asked.

She nodded, her eyes still damp, but the storm in them seemed to have passed.

She offered him a teary smile.

"Good," he said, his voice steady. "Are you hungry?" She shook her head, and he didn't press.

Instead, he offered her a handkerchief, his thumb grazing the back of her hand as she took it. The simple gesture was a small comfort; one he hoped would ease the tension between them.

He waited as she wiped her face, giving her the space to collect herself.

When she was done, he didn't hesitate. He bent down, his strong arms lifting her effortlessly, cradling her against him.

Without a word, he carried her across the room, his strides

purposeful yet gentle.

Lowering her onto the couch with a tenderness that spoke volumes, he sat beside her, close enough that she could feel his warmth, but not forcing her into anything she wasn't ready for.

* * *

"Tseye?" It was a question; he turned to face her as she smiled at him.

She touched his hand;

"Thank you," she said and then she leaned forward and kissed him.

Chapter Twenty-One

Eight Months Later

Zala's hands trembled slightly as she surveyed the scene before her.

She couldn't help but feel the weight of the moment; everything had to be perfect. Today was Tseye's birthday, and she had taken the day off work to prepare dinner.

She knew he would be surprised as he wasn't expecting to see her till tomorrow evening.

She glanced nervously at the decorations, the flowers, the candles, all carefully arranged, but her doubts lingered.

"Relax, Zala," Yahimba said. She walked over with a smile, standing before her with hands on her hips. "It's perfect. You've done a great job."

Zala hesitated, looking around. "You think so?"

Yahimba laughed lightly, her eyes glinting with humor. "I

know. I helped you; I cooked most of the dishes," she teased, her playful smirk lifting the tension in the air.

Zala couldn't help but chuckle and shake her head.

"You're too much," Zala said, the hint of a smile tugging at the corner of her lips.

Yahimba's expression softened, her gaze shifting to something more serious as she checked her watch. "Eyimofe is downstairs, you're okay, right? Can I leave now? We have to meet his mom for the cake tasting," she asked, glancing up at Zala with a look of mild concern.

"I'm fine," Zala replied quickly, brushing a few stray strands of hair behind her ear. "Go ahead. Let me know how it goes."

Yahimba smiled warmly and gave her a quick hug. "You've got this, Zala. I'll call you later."

Two months had passed since Eyimofe and Yahimba had gotten engaged, and plans were already moving forward at full speed. The wedding date was set, and Tseye was over the moon about his sister marrying his best friend. Zala couldn't help but feel a flicker of happiness for them both, but also a quiet pang in her chest.

It was a reminder of how far she'd come and yet how much she still held back.

* * *

Tseye's lips curved into a wide grin as he stepped into the foyer, his eyes lighting up when he saw Zala walking out of the kitchen. "I wasn't expecting you," he said, his voice rich with surprise and delight.

Zala's smile was bright and playful as she walked to- ward him. "It's your birthday; how could I possibly miss it?" She wrapped her arms around his neck, tilting her head up to kiss him.

Tseye's heart gave a soft thud as he dropped his keys on the console table, his hands instinctively moving to gather her into his arms.

Their lips met in a tender kiss, full of love, the kind that felt like it could last forever.

"Good surprise," he whispered against her lips, his voice low and warm, a hint of lust in his gaze.

Zala pulled back just slightly, blushing at the look in his eyes. "I cooked Nigerian dishes," she said, her smile full of pride.

Tseye raised an eyebrow, clearly impressed. "You cooked?" he asked, the surprise evident in his voice.

Zala nodded, her grin widening. "Yahimba helped, of course. But I can cook," she said, a teasing edge to her voice. "I have to learn more Nigerian recipes if I'm going to keep up with you."

He laughed, the sound genuine and full of affection. "I'm

impressed," he said, following her into the living room. There, spread out on the table, was a beautiful array of fragrant, vibrant, and colorful Nigerian dishes, each plate

a little slice of home.

"This looks amazing," he said. "Remind me to thank Yahimba for helping you."

"I hope you are hungry," she chuckled.

"I am," Tseye replied, his smile widening as he leaned in to kiss her. "And I'm even hungrier for you."

Zala laughed softly, a light flush coloring her cheeks, her heart fluttering at his words.

"You're impossible," she teased, though the warmth in her voice said she didn't mind.

"I know," he said with a wink, pulling out a chair for her. "But only for you."

* * *

After dinner, they moved into the living room, the qui- et hum of the evening settling around them as they tidied up together.

The faint scent of the meal lingered in the air, but Zala's mind was elsewhere.

She was nervous as usual, but this was good.

She watched as Tseye settled onto the couch and patted the space next to him, an unspoken invitation for her to join him.

But she declined.

Instead, she picked up a cushion and positioned it in front of him.

Then, slowly, she knelt before him, bringing her face to eye level with his. Her heart raced, but there was a resolve in her chest. This was a moment she had been putting off for far too long.

And she had prepared for it.

"What are you doing?" Tseye's voice was amused. His lips curled into a smile as he watched her adjust the top she wore.

Zala met his gaze, her eyes full of warmth but also a hint of vulnerability.

"Gathering the courage to seduce you," she said softly.

He laughed, the sound rich and affectionate, and gently touched her cheek.

"Babe, you seduce me just by being here," he said, his fingers trailing softly along her skin, sending a shiver down her spine.

Not that kind of seduction, she wanted to say.

That kind of seduction would come later.

This, she had to do alone, and suddenly, all the nervousness she felt disappeared.

She was ready.

"I know," she whispered, her gaze never leaving his.

Tseye leaned back slightly, his expression softening as he watched her. "So, what are we doing?"

Zala took a deep breath, her fingers trembling slightly as she reached forward and pressed her lips gently to his, as though kissing him was the only thing that could steady the storm raging in her chest.

When she pulled away, she whispered, her voice thick with emotion, "I love you, Tseye Harriman."

His eyes softened, and his smile widened. "I love you more," he murmured, brushing a strand of hair away from her face.

Zala closed her eyes briefly, gathering the strength to say the words that had been weighing on her heart for so long. When she spoke again, her voice was quieter, more fragile. "No, let me speak, please." She took a deep breath, feeling the weight of the confession settle within her.

He had to know.

She had to tell him how she felt.

"These last months… I have watched you. I have seen you support me, be there for me, hold me when I cry, and laugh when I'm happy. You've helped me heal in ways I never thought possible." Her breath caught as she paused, searching his face for some sign of understanding. "I can't imagine spending my life without you, Tseye. I don't want to. You make me feel whole, you make me feel safe."

Her heart thundered in her chest, and her hands shook as she reached into her pocket. Slowly, she pulled out a small velvet box and held it out to him.

For a moment, she couldn't breathe.

This was it, the moment she had been fearing and yearning for all at once.

She opened the box, revealing the delicate ring inside, a simple gold band that glinted in the light.

"Tseye Harriman," she whispered, her voice cracking slightly with emotion, "Will you marry me and make me the happiest woman in the world?"

* * *

Tseye's heart slammed against his chest as his eyes landed on the gold band nestled inside the small velvet box.

For a moment, time seemed to freeze.

His mind raced, unable to fully process what he was seeing. Zala had just proposed. The weight of what she had just done hit him all at once, and his breath caught in his throat. His eyes met hers, wide with emotion, and the sight of her bright tears mirrored his own.

The air around them felt charged with emotions as if the entire world had paused to witness this moment.

He could hardly believe it!

Without thinking, he hurled her into his arms with such force that they fell back into the sofa, pressing her body against his as if he could somehow pull the moment into him.

His lips found hers in a fierce, desperate kiss, filled with all the love, longing, and relief he'd kept buried for so long.

"God, yes! Yes! I will marry you!" he muttered against her lips, his voice rough with emotion. Then, he pulled back just enough to look into her eyes. His heart swelled as he saw her smiling through her tears. "I will marry you, Zala. A thousand times, yes. I love you so much."

And then, rolling her beneath him, he kissed her, slowly at first, as though testing the waters, delighting in her response; they kissed with a growing intensity that mirrored the surge of emotions between them.

His lips brushed against hers, soft and tentative, before deepening. His hands threaded through her hair, pulling her closer.

He loved Zala; everything about her delighted him; every

touch and movement was a silent confession of everything he'd been holding back.

This was what he wanted; this was where he wanted to be.

With Zala, no barriers, no walls. Just Zala.

Epilogue

Ikoyi, Lagos Nigeria

When I had taken the steps to move to Lagos, I had no idea what to expect.

I had no idea what life had in store for me.

Broken, scarred, and depressed, the only thing that kept me going was Zuri, my daughter.

Then Tseye Harriman came back into my life.

After what I did to him, how I treated him, Tseye was still willing to be with me.

My best friend My cheerleader My lover

My fiancée

Tseye is everything to me and more.

He accepts me just as I am, holding my hands when I cry and laughing with me when I laugh.

Tseye Harriman helped me heal. He made me believe in myself.

Because of him, I know I am not a victim. Because of him, I can love, be loved and give love. I am Zala Kebede, soon to be Zala Harriman.

Scarred by love, I have learnt to love and be loved.

EXCERPT FROM OBEYI'S STORY COMING AUTUMN 2025

Prologue

London, United Kingdom

I am furious.

The news of my so-called engagement is splashed across

The Lagos Diaries.

My parents, undeterred by my refusals, have gone ahead and announced my marriage to Naade Adekoya-Phillips.

I clench my fists, fighting back the tears threatening to spill.

How could they disregard my wishes so completely?

I fled to London a week ago to escape this fate, making it abundantly clear that I would never marry Naade, that arrogant, two-faced philanderer!

And yet, here I am, caught in a nightmare I have tried so

hard to avoid.

My heart tightens as I think about why I came here in the first place, I came to meet Ade. The man I have loved for two years. The man who shattered me just weeks ago with the cruelest confession: he never saw me as wife material, I wasn't good enough for him.

I should have seen it coming.

His behavior changed after I lost the baby two months ago. I had been filled with joy at the pregnancy, believing it would bring us closer together. Instead, it drove a wedge be- tween us. The miscarriage only deepened the divide, leaving me feeling hollow, broken, and now, he says that "I Obehi Okoduwa is not good enough to be his wife"

As if that wasn't enough, my parents have decided to force me into an engagement with a man who detests me as much as I detest him.

Naade Adekoya-Phillips. I've had enough.

Enough of rejection.

Enough of being pushed into relationships that leave me shattered.

It's time for me to take control of my life, embracing my dreams, my happiness, and the future I deserve.

I will. I must.

I am Obehi Okoduwa.

Acknowledgements

E very time I finish a story, I find myself with a long list of incredible people to thank.

First and foremost, I am deeply grateful for the unwavering support and encouragement that allows me to continue crafting stories that resonate.

To Iteno Omoruku and Tobore Moruku, thank you for always being in my corner, cheering me on to the finish line and generously sharing ideas that help shape my work. Your belief in me is invaluable.

A special thanks to Sutapa Mondal for their brilliant contributions to my books. Your dedication and talent elevate my stories, and I couldn't have done this without you.

To my husband, Uyavie, you are my greatest source of inspiration. Thank you for believing in me, for your constant encouragement, and for always being my rock.

Finally, to my dearest readers, you are the heart of it all. Your love and enthusiasm for my stories inspire me to keep writing. Thank you for being part of this journey and for bringing my words to life with your imaginations.

With profound gratitude,

O.L Obonna

About the Author

O.L. Obonna was born in Lagos, Nigeria, and has always had a passion for storytelling. She loves creating romantic stories filled with emotion, excitement, and unforgettable characters. Through her writing, she brings readers into captivating worlds of love, family, friendship, and drama.

Her stories blend romance, charm, and mystery, offering readers heartfelt and engaging experiences that stay with them long after the final page.

In addition to writing, O.L. Obonna is also passionate about publishing and sharing meaningful stories that readers can connect with. When she is not writing, publishing, or reading romance novels, she enjoys trying out new recipes and painting with her children.

She lives in London with her husband and their three children.

Connect with O.L. Obonna

- Website: www.inkbyolobonna.com

- Instagram: @inkbyolobonna

- X: @inkbyolobonna

she can't resist!

Still recovering from a heartbreaking and painful loss, Yahimba leaves everything and everyone she knows and moves across the country, determined to put the past behind her. However, she didn't anticipate getting the attention of Eyimofe Alele-Williams, her brother's best friend. Handsome and charming, Eyimofe is the kind of man she knows she could easily fall in love with. But she's been hurt by love before and has no interest in risking her heart again. However, their connection might be too strong. It is a fire that threatens to consume her, igniting a passion she never knew she had. Despite her misgivings about him, Yahimba is left wondering what if? She must grapple with her emotions and decide if she's ready to take the plunge and give in to her feelings for him.

Burned by Love, can she learn to love and trust again?

Or would it be safer to walk away?

A SNEAK PEEK OF KISS ME GOODNIGHT IN ROME

Mia

"What about this?" I ask my friends, smoothing my hands over my hips.

Maura, Lila, and Emma lounge around my bedroom in New York, assessing my wardrobe and offering advice. I study my reflection, biting my lip. The dress is black, knee-length, with a square neckline and thick straps. It's classy yet understated. I wore it to the Junior-Senior dance showcase during my sophomore year at McShain University.

Lila tosses her long blond waves over her shoulder, her eyes crinkling. "You're kidding me, right?"

"What's wrong with it? Oh, jeez, is the neckline too low?" I tug it up higher.

"You look like you're going to a funeral." Emma points at me.

Glancing at Maura, she nods.

Epic fail. How the hell am I supposed to embrace the college pact if I can't even look the part? I've never stepped out of my comfort zone before and after months of watching my life implode, I'm ready for a change. I need an adventure, an experience…something to remind me that I'm going to be okay.

"Don't question Emma, Mia. She may not be right about everything," Lila says, blowing a kiss in Emma's direction, "but when it comes to fashion, take her advice and run with it."

"Mia, you're going to Italy, the epicenter of fashion. Embrace it. Wear colors and try new things. Rome is not some stuffy ballet theater." Emma stands next to me. Squeezing my shoulder in the reflection of the mirror, she grins. "It's … well, it's everything."

"What does that even mean?" Maura raises a sculpted eyebrow.

"It means that this," Emma indicates my black dress, "isn't going to cut it for Rome. Luckily I brought some options. Nothing too crazy," she clarifies as I open my mouth to protest, "just a few staples." She moves to her overnight bag, pulling out an armful of clothing.

"Yes!" Lila claps her hands. "This is perfect for the pact, Mia." Lila takes some articles of clothing from Emma, spreading them out on my bed. "You promised," she adds as if I could forget an agreement I made only hours ago.

"Date tall, dark, and handsomes," Maura recalls, rolling her eyes as she references Lila's favorite topic: boys.

"Obviously. And have an epic senior year. Being adventurous, embracing the moment, making sure we have no regrets," Lila summarizes. "We all agreed."

We did all agree. We made a pact to have a wild, adventurous, exciting senior year – stepping out of our comfort zones, pushing the envelope, bending the rules. We raised our glasses and drank to this new journey.

Except I'm the ultimate rule follower and the thought of

being wild gives me hives. The fear of moving to Rome tomorrow morning for my study abroad is thick in my throat, causing my tongue to stick. Thoughts ricochet in my mind, rendering me unable to respond to Emma's fashion suggestions as she holds up her basic staples or meet Lila's eyes as she chatters about Italian men and Ferraris.

Except I need this pact. I need this change. For too long, I've been stuck. Now, I'm twenty-one-years-old and I don't know how to flirt, mingle, and make small talk. I have no clue how to fill my time after so many years adhering to my strict ballet schedule. I've never traded study sessions in the library for nights out with the girls.

I understand discipline, dedication, and organization. Without my friends, without ballet and the familiarity of McShain's campus, I'm not sure I know how to…be.

But God, do I want to.

Maura offers a sympathetic smile. "I'm really proud of you for doing this, for being brave. And I know your mom is looking down on you smiling that you're taking this trip. Trust me, it's going to be worth it."

An unexpected swell of emotion bubbles in my throat. *I can do this. I can be a person who learns how to have free time. And enjoy it. Can't I?*

"And your black dress is practical," Maura adds.

"Thanks." My fingers fidget over the lines of my dress. In the mirror, my straight brown hair falls limply to my shoulders. Sucking in my stomach, it barely moves. My thick, fleshy thighs expand before my eyes. I blink.

My face is pasty pale with two dull, void eyes staring back. All sparkle vanished after I lost ballet, which snuffed out my future dreams and shattered my heart. Closing my eyes so I don't have to stare at all my imperfections simultaneously, I count to ten.

But when I open them, my bland expression, bloated stomach, and boring black dress are still there.

Yes, I need this. It's time for a change. A life makeover.

"It's the new you!" Emma exclaims, reading my thoughts. She unzips the back of my dress and it slides down my body, pooling around my feet like a waterfall. "Seriously, Mia, if I had your figure, I would definitely flaunt it a bit more. You're one of the lucky ones, everything looks amazing on you. So do us thicker girls a favor and slut it up a bit. Here, put this one on." She hands me a short, olive green sweater dress. "I stole it from my sister, so there's a tiny chance it will actually fit you and not just hang off your limbs."

Pulling the dress over my head, I smooth it down my frame.

"Pair it with tights and these boots." Emma holds up a pair of brown leather boots with a chunky heel. "They're comfy. Swear it." She tosses the boots into my open suitcase.

"Oh, you are going to turn heads and break hearts, Mia Petrella!" Lila shouts, picking up a bottle of wine she deposited on my desk hours ago. Digging into her purse, her hand exits with a corkscrew. She opens the bottle, takes a long swig, and passes it to me. "I bet you even lose your virginity."

Rolling my eyes, I lift a hand to stop my friends before they can launch into —

"It's not that there's anything wrong with being a virgin," Emma says slowly.

"Not at all. It's just, who could be better than an Italian for her first time?" Lila asks as if there is no possible comparison.

"True," Emma agrees.

Maura swipes the bottle from my hand and chugs. Her newly discovered appreciation for wine, or alcohol in general, is evident when she smacks her lips. "I'm kind of jealous you're going to drink this nectar from the gods like the rest of us drink water. If you do decide to cash in your V-card, make sure you drink several bottles first."

"Maura!" Emma tugs on Maura's long, curly hair and shakes her head. Looking at me, she smiles. "She's exaggerating. While the first time may be uncomfortable, it's not like, excruciatingly painful."

"Guys, it's fine. Honestly, I need this. The pact, the adventure, the hot guys. I'm turning over a new leaf. Mia Petrella, the ballerina, is done. It's time to invent a new me."

"Hell yeah, girl! You are going to slay. I would do the first man who called me *bella*." Lila places her hand over her heart. "You look hot. I like this color on you."

"There's more!" Emma holds up a pile of sweaters, depositing them in my suitcase.

"Rome is going to be amazing. Think of all the sexy Italian men you're going to meet. I bet they're all tall, dark, and handsome," Lila sighs, twirling around my bedroom.

"I never thought I'd say this, Li, but I'm ready to meet them all." I hold up the wine bottle, tip it back, and take a large gulp.

Liquid courage.

I'm going to embrace this.

Ciao a Roma.

ALSO BY GINA AZZI

The College Pact Series:

The Last First Game (Lila's Story)

All the While (Maura's Story)

Me + You (Emma's Story)

Kiss Me Goodnight in Rome (Mia's Story)

The Regretful Lies Duet:

Broken Lies

Twisted Truths

Spinoff:

Saving My Soul (Coming September 16)

Healing My Heart (Charlie's Story - 2020)

The Kane Brothers Series:

Rescuing Broken (Jax's Story)

Recovering Beauty (Carter's Story)

Reclaiming Brave (Denver's Story)

My Christmas Wish

(A Kane Family Christmas

+ *One Last Chance* FREE prequel)

Finding Love in Scotland Series:

My Christmas Wish

(A Kane Family Christmas

Young Adult Standalone:

ABOUT THE AUTHOR

Gina Azzi writes Contemporary Romance with relatable, genuine characters experiencing real life love, friendships, and challenges. She is the author of The Kane Brothers Series, The College Pact Series (re-launching summer 2019), and Corner of Ocean and Bay. All of her books can be read as stand-alones.

A Jersey girl at heart, Gina has spent her twenties traveling the world, living and working abroad, before settling down in Ontario, Canada with her husband and three children. She's a voracious reader, daydreamer, and coffee enthusiast who loves meeting new people. Say hey to her on social media or through www.ginaazzi.com.

For more information, connect with Gina at:

Email: ginaazziauthor@gmail.com
Twitter: @gina_azzi
Instagram: @gina_azzi
Facebook: https://www.facebook.com/ginaazziauthor
Website: www.ginaazzi.com

Or subscribe to her newsletter to receive book updates, bonus content, and more!

Misan's free and unbothered laughter rang out. "Oh, I'm coming for your wedding, Naade. I can't wait for you to get married. What is it you guys call yourselves again? The Lagos Elite Club!" She grinned, her eyes dancing with mischief. "Finally, we will have a wedding with real drama."

"You two are impossible," Naade muttered under his breath, shaking his head.

Tseye, not missing a beat, smirked and said to Misan. "I'm buying your ticket,"

Misan winked. "You better."

"Oh, I will; we have to support Naade and make sure he gets married," Tseye said, laughing.

Chapter Twenty

"**B**ut just so you know, you're not going anywhere until we've had that talk."

His words lingered in her mind, echoing like a subtle warning as she stood quietly, watching Naade and Tseye conversing with his sister, Yahimba.

The weight of his words still hung between them. Was she ready for that talk?

Her eyes flicked between Tseye and Yahimba, her thoughts clouded.

He told her to " just wait" while he and Naade arranged for a driver to take his sister home.

It seemed like such a small thing, yet the way Tseye had said it, with that calm authority, made her pulse quicken; it had been weeks since they had spoken, and she knew Tseye was determined to talk to her.

The question was: Was she ready to talk?